SHANE

The Mavericks, Book 12

Dale Mayer

SHANE: THE MAVERICKS, BOOK 12
Dale Mayer
Valley Publishing Ltd.

ISBN-13: 978-1-773363-77-6
Print Edition

Books in This Series:

About This Book

What happens when the very men—trained to make the hard decisions—come up against the rules and regulations that hold them back from doing what needs to be done? They either stay and work within the constraints given to them or they walk away. Only now, for a select few, they have another option:

The Mavericks. A covert black ops team that steps up and break all the rules … but gets the job done.

Welcome to a new military romance series by *USA Today* best-selling author Dale Mayer. A series where you meet new friends and just might get to meet old ones too in this raw and compelling look at the men who keep us safe every day from the darkness where they operate—and live—in the shadows … until someone special helps them step into the light.

Her kidnappers demanded Shane arrive. Finding out his best friend was held as a pawn just pissed him off. Finding out rescuing her was a test made him seriously angry. He hates being used. These men mean business though, as Shane finds a body count too high for comfort.

Shelly knew Shane would come for her. No way he wouldn't. She was lucky to have Shane there for her, especially when learning a second woman had been kidnapped and held for over six months. The simple rescue of Shelly turns into something more to find this second woman.

But is there one killer boss out there or two? As the pair try to secure their own freedom, it gets even murkier, until finding a way through is paramount. Otherwise no one gets a happy ending.

Sign up to be notified of all Dale's releases here!

https://smarturl.it/DaleNews

PROLOGUE

S HANE ANDREWS OPENED his apartment door, walked inside, and tossed his duffel bag down. He headed to the fridge, pulled out a cold beer, and stepped out on his small deck. He popped the top and took a long refreshing drink. That had been one hell of a job in Hawaii. A lot of healing needed to happen now for that family. Not only did the parents have to heal but the children and the grandchildren were involved as well. He didn't understand Melinda being so self-centered, so selfish that she would put her parents and her sister through so much, just to make sure she got what she wanted.

Melinda had been a piece of work. That she'd been a suspect right from the beginning didn't surprise Shane, just because her attitude had been so off. But the fact that Steve had been a willing party to it all was too much, especially considering that he was a navy man Shane should have been able to trust.

He rotated his neck, stretching out some of the kinks. It had been a long two days. He was home now and needed a few days to regroup. At least he hoped he got a couple days off. He'd taken an extra day to stay with Gavin and the family to tie up things and to get all the facts straight.

Now that Shane was home, he didn't know quite what the next few days would bring, but he was up for it. At least he thought he would be. It was a hell of a deal joining the Mavericks, but he was pretty happy with his decision. If ever somebody needed to be stopped, it was Melinda. He hadn't expected this to be the level of the work he would be doing. Still, it was what it was.

As he sat here, his phone buzzed, and he smiled when he saw it was Gavin. He hit the Talk button. "I'm home, safe and sound, bud. No need to worry about me."

"Hey, I just wanted to make sure you were looking after that leg of yours," he said.

"Yep, we're all good."

"Good," he said. "How do you feel about New York?"

"Why in the hell would I ever want to go there?" he asked.

At that, Gavin laughed. "Remember Diesel?"

"Diesel Edwards? Yeah, I remember. What about him?"

"He'll be waiting for you there at the airport."

"Shit, am I leaving already?" Shane asked, as he looked at his beer.

"Absolutely. Well, in about three hours," he said.

"Wow, not even enough time to do a load of laundry."

"Sure there is. If you just put down that beer, get up off your ass, and get your clothes in the machine," Gavin said, laughing, "you can drink it while they wash."

"So, what am I doing in New York?" he asked, as he walked to grab his bag of dirty clothes and did exactly that. With the washing machine started, he grabbed his beer and looked down at his phone. "What is it you aren't saying?"

"It looks like a hostage situation has gone down in a big telecom building," he said.

"What's that got to do with me?"

"Well, Diesel is already in position, or he will be soon.

He'll pick you up at the airport. You are going into the tunnels and coming up through the basement."

"What the hell does SWAT have to say about that?"

"Well, they're hoping this might be right up your alley."

"Why is that?"

"Because, uh, … because one of your best friends is in there."

At that moment, everything inside Shane froze.

"Shelly?" He remembered her saying she had a brand-new job in New York. "I know she just moved there, but what's she doing in the telecom building?"

"She was a new hire about forty-five days ago," he said. "Didn't you hear about it?"

And, of course, he had, but he had completely forgotten. "Why do you think she's involved? That's a huge building."

"Because the kidnappers said she was. And they are hanging on to her until you arrive. So get your ass out there."

CHAPTER 1

S HANE DISEMBARKED FROM the plane carrying his duffel bag over his shoulder and tried to work around what had to be several thousand people between him and the exit. They all had to get past the luggage turnstiles. Finally catching a break as the crowd parted, Shane worked his way through, headed for the exit. Once outside, he stopped and took several long slow deep breaths. The air here was never the same as it was back in California. New York always had more smog, a heavier atmosphere, and that smell. Mostly traffic exhaust, as far as he could ever tell. Then that sense of being rushed.

He walked to the curb, where he took a closer look at the vehicles up and down the street. Diesel was supposed to be here waiting for him, at least that's the last word he'd gotten from Gavin. Just as he was about to turn and look back the other way, he heard a shout. He spun and looked on the far side of the street down about ten cars to see a tall beef of a man standing outside his truck and waving at him.

Checking the traffic, Shane quickly dodged through the oncoming vehicles and headed toward his old friend. As soon as he got there, Diesel's grin flashed.

"Damn, man," Diesel said, "it's good to see you." The two high-fived each other, as Shane tossed his duffel bag into the open pickup bed, then scrambled into the passenger seat.

"Why does it always take chaos or something like this to bring us together?"

"Well, if we had any more chaos," Diesel said, "we would be damn near living on top of each other."

"Isn't that the truth," Shane said, grumping. "I just finished a big case with Gavin," he murmured, "and was hoping for a few days off."

"You'd have gotten it," Diesel said, "except for the fact that the kidnappers have a friend of yours."

"I know. I can't believe she got herself into trouble already," he said, shaking his head. "I swear. Every time she turns around, she somehow manages to find some."

"Sounds like you know her pretty well."

"I do," he said. "We've been friends since kindergarten."

At that, Diesel burst out laughing. "Seriously?" He looked at Shane, thinking he was exaggerating, but Shane was serious.

He nodded. "I'm not kidding. Man, that woman could get herself and anybody nearby in trouble so fast that you didn't know what hit you."

"How is she at getting out of trouble?"

"She's got some uncanny luck," he said. "I mean that too. How else does she manage to get somebody like me for something like this?"

"Well, this case might not be a very good example."

"Okay, fine," he said, "but it wouldn't matter. Something or someone else would have come to her rescue."

"Interesting," Diesel said. "I don't think I've ever heard you mention her."

"That's because we don't come in contact that often," he said, "but she's one of those long-term friends you can pick up a phone and call out of the blue, no matter how many years have gone by."

"Those are the special ones."

"Exactly," he said. "So I'm still figuring out the background. Did you get any news from Gavin on it?"

"The kidnappers aren't talking. It sounds like maybe they've got some beef with you, and either they snagged her after finding out who she was or gave her the job down there in the hopes that you would visit, but, when you didn't appear fast enough, they orchestrated this scenario to get you here."

"Jesus. Who have I pissed off lately? Well," he said, laughing bitterly, "who haven't I?"

"Right," Diesel said. "No shortage of people on the wrong side of our world."

"What about Hawaii? Do you think it had anything to do with that?" he asked Diesel. "How much do you know about that case?"

"I only know the quick version," he said, "but Gavin doesn't seem to think it's connected."

"Well, I'll go with his gut on that for now," he said.

"What kind of work does Shelly do?"

"Project management," he said. Then he chuckled. "Shelly is really good at ordering people around."

Diesel shook his head. "I'm glad you say that with a smile on your face, but I can't tell if you're teasing or not."

"No, she's very good at telling people what to do and where to go," he said, "but maybe she's tempered that for her work. I don't know. She was always a fairly reckless kid growing up, and we got along famously. I'd push. She'd shove, and we'd end up on the ground, wrestling and pulling each other's hair. She never wanted to be treated like a girl, and, at the same time, she's the most feminine-looking angel you ever saw."

"She sounds like a tough little nut."

"Yes, she was, right up until her mother died from breast cancer," he said quickly. "After that, she became a different person. As if all that fighting and bickering may have been to prove herself to her mother or something. I don't know," he said. "Her father died when she was about five, somewhere around the time that I met her. She was a really sad little kid back then. I befriended her, not sure exactly why, but something about her caused my heart to ache. We've been buddies ever since."

"But only buddies?"

"Yep, only buddies," he said. "I've called her up a number of times to commemorate when I've broken up from relationships, and she's done the same. We've often killed a case of beer or crushed some Häagen-Dazs in memory of the relationships that no longer were."

"I'm surprised you guys didn't get together," Diesel said.

"We discussed it once," he said, "and, in all honesty, we decided we needed our friendship more." He grinned at Diesel. "So that goes to tell you how well we communicate."

"That's amazing," he murmured. He wove through traffic, taking the vehicle from one end of town to the other.

"So what the hell is going on with this communication company? What do they know about me?"

"I don't know. Check in with Gavin to see if they've got any updates. My understanding was that the kidnappers said they would talk to you and only you."

"They didn't say what they wanted, huh?"

"Nope. Everybody's in the dark about that."

"Great," he said. "These deals are always the craziest, no idea which way to go or where to run."

"Exactly, which is why they think you're arriving in six hours on a different flight."

"Nice. So we've got a six-hour window then." Shane rubbed his hands together. "Are we well equipped?"

"Anything you want, you better speak up," Diesel said, "because six hours won't give us that much time. But, generally with Gavin, whatever we need, we'll get."

"I hope so," Shane said, "because I don't want to go into something like this without hefty firepower."

"No, I agree with you there. Especially not knowing just what we're up against."

"Yeah, and that'll be a little hard to figure out."

"Absolutely. Give Gavin a shout, and see what he knows."

Shane pulled out his phone and quickly sent off a text to Gavin. "Do we have a hotel yet?"

"Yeah, we're heading there right now," Diesel said. "It's a small three-star hotel around the corner from the communication office."

"Perfect. Any tunnels under there?"

"Yeah," he said, "but just the underground city tunnels. The ones that feed in and out to access the sewer lines and subways."

"Great," he said. "We'll need some extra protective gear then."

"Absolutely. Make a list of everything you want, including the firepower."

Almost in delight, Shane pulled out a notepad and wrote down what he thought he would need. When he was done, he read it aloud to Diesel. "I'm not even sure we can carry all this stuff."

"Well, not only carry it but we may have to squeeze into

some pretty narrow places," he said. "I don't know what it's like down there in sewer city."

"It's tight," Shane said. "I've been in a couple, but not New York's though."

"We've got the maps already. So we'll just make a quick stop at the hotel to check in, drop off our stuff, then pick up what we need and move out."

"Good. Hopefully Shelly and I will be sitting over a steak later tonight."

"Well, that would be ideal. I'm not sure if I, uh, if I'm welcome to join you or not," he said, "but a steak sounds like a pretty decent way to end the day."

"Absolutely," Shane said. "Besides, you never know. You guys might hit it off."

Diesel looked at him, smiled, and said, "We'll see about that." As they pulled up to the hotel, he said, "Go ahead and check in, Shane. I'll go switch to a different vehicle, and I'll be right back."

"Okay. What name is the reservation under?"

"Mine," he said.

With that, Shane hopped out, grabbed his duffel bag, and walked inside. As soon as he was in the hotel room, he brought out his laptop and quickly opened up the Mavericks chat box and typed in the list of needs he had made. The response came back quickly.

Two hours.

Shane replied immediately. **Make it an hour and fifteen. We're short on time.**

He brought up the online map of the underground tunnels they would need to access in order to get into the telecom building and figured it would take them about an hour to navigate that too. Which meant they were really pushed for time. He took a quick shower and got out just as Diesel arrived.

"The equipment should be coming in less than an hour," Shane said. "I figure it will take us an hour to navigate the tunnels and up into the building. What we need to know is where exactly they're holding her in there."

"And that's a possibility," he said. "We're expecting a phone call from them."

Shane looked at him with surprise. "From the kidnappers?"

"Yes." Diesel checked his watch and said, "In about five minutes."

"Good, let's get set up for that then."

SHELLY BERKSHIRE GLARED at her kidnappers. "He won't come. You know that, right?"

They ignored her, just like they had ignored her every other time that she'd brought it up. She'd been initially terrified, but, as soon as she realized they were after Shane, her anger grew. Of course their comment about her being his doxy set it aflame.

She hoped Shane didn't come. It seemed like he was always bailing her out of these things. Although she hadn't done a single thing to bring this one on, so it wasn't her fault. She figured somebody hated him already, and they were using her for bait somehow. She watched the clock, knowing a phone call was supposed to happen. And she would probably speak, would be proof of life.

If she knew anything about Shane, he would make sure she was okay. The problem was, she needed to have some message ready in order to give him some help. Even if they got into the building somehow, it was massive, and she couldn't tell him a whole lot, not with her kidnappers listening in.

She had thought about it long and hard, thinking about where they'd been all their life and how she'd ended up in this stupid scenario. She knew the job offer had been too good to believe. Although nobody would have expected her boss to take a bullet between the eyes, as these guys came through the building. Assholes. She didn't know who else or how many other people had been killed in the process, but what was driving her nuts was why they had chosen this route to get her. And it drove her crazy. Not only was she a sitting duck and completely in the middle of this but all of it was done to hurt Shane. And that was horrible. He was her best friend and had been since forever.

Just then the two gunmen got up, synced their watches, and made a phone call to somebody else.

Her heart slammed in her chest. This was it. Then they came over and, grabbing her under each arm, half-lifted and half-carried her to the boardroom, sitting off to the right of this room. It was a conference room with just tables and chairs. A laptop was brought up, which she kept her eyes on, before she realized that a video was on a larger screen up in the front. And, sure enough, there was Shane. She feasted on his familiar face and gave him a teary smile in return.

"Are you okay?" he asked gruffly.

She nodded; her heart warmed that he would actually come. "You shouldn't have come. You know that, right?"

He gave her a lopsided grin. "If our positions were reversed—"

"I'd leave you in the mess you made," she said.

He burst out laughing, until the laptop was jerked away from her face.

"Now that you know she's alive," the gunman said, "we want you here, and we want you here in the next forty minutes."

"I can't make that," he said. "Make it two hours. That's the soonest I can get there. I'm sure you've already figured out that I've just now landed."

"Forty minutes should be enough time."

"No way," he said, "so it's two hours or nothing."

"Well, maybe it'll be nothing then," the one man snarled. He slammed Shelly's head into view again. "We don't have to wait for you to hurt this one."

"Well, I suggest you don't," Shane said, his voice turning hard. "Even the slightest bruise on her skin, and I'll make sure it's ten times worse on whoever gave it to her."

The man laughed. "We don't care what you think you'll do. We just want you here."

"Got it," he said. "Two hours." He looked back at her and asked, "Shelly, are you okay?"

"I'm okay," she said, then she took a deep breath. "Remember back at Smithville?"

She didn't get a chance to finish. Her head was jerked off to the side again, and a hand clapped over her mouth.

"That's all she says," the man growled. "Now hurry up and get here." And, with that, the screen went black. As soon as it did, he turned and smacked her hard across the face.

She cried out at the stinging blow that sent her head snapping to the side.

"I don't know what you were trying to do," he said, "but no more tricks. I mean it."

She didn't say anything, her head still ringing from the

pain. She wanted to slap him back even harder. She had some self-defense skills, but she was up against at least two of them, if not four, the others off somewhere else, and they were each very well-armed, and she wasn't. She wasn't averse to taking a chance if there was any hope, but these guys looked to not give a damn if they killed her or not. "You still haven't explained why you're doing this," she murmured.

"Don't have to explain anything," he snapped.

She nodded. "No, that's true," she said. "You don't, but it would sure make it easier for me to understand what's going on if you would. That's all."

"He did something wrong. He needs to pay for it," the other man said, and it was the first time she had heard him speak.

She looked at him in surprise. "He did?"

He looked at her, nodded, and said, "You seem surprised."

"I've never known him to hurt anybody," she said quietly. "He's the opposite."

"Not in this instance," he said.

"Shut up now," the leader said, as he stood and looked at the other two. "Joe and Pete, you guys stay here, and don't let her say another word. Not one." They just nodded and took up positions in chairs near her.

Joe and Pete, huh? She looked at the leader. "Who are you?" she asked. "Shouldn't I at least know who orchestrated the last few hours of my life?"

"You can call me Bruce," he said, with a ghost of a smile. "And you might live through this yet," he said. "You're only a means to an end. We don't have any beef with you. Best you not give us one."

"So this is all just to get to Shane?"

"Absolutely," he said, "and, after we've got him, you can leave. We'll let you go," he said. And, with a smile, he turned and walked out.

But absolutely nothing in that smile made her believe him. As a matter of fact, she was pretty damn sure he had lied. They wouldn't let her go. No way.

CHAPTER 2

S HELLY SETTLED BACK in the corner. She'd been allowed to move over there, so she could rest her head back. Other than that, she was left in silence. She wanted to ask a million questions, but there just didn't seem to be anything she could do. Her mind spun endlessly, figuring out a way to get out of here. Just then another woman was shoved into the room with her. She looked up to see Mary, an older coworker, her face flushed and her hands shaking, as she fell slightly, catching herself on the table. Immediately Shelly hopped up and hurried to her. "Are you okay?"

Mary looked at her worriedly. "What's going on?" she asked. "What do these men want?"

"They want somebody I know," she said quietly. "Apparently they took me captive in order to bring him here."

"Why?" Mary wailed. "I just saw Mr. Markham. He was such a nice man."

"I know, and he didn't deserve this," she said quietly.

At that, Mary started to cry. "It's just terrible," she said.

"Did they say why you're here, Mary?"

"No," she said. "I just wanted to go home."

"Did you ask to go home?"

"No," she said. "I didn't think they would listen to me."

"Probably not," she said, her tone sympathetic. "They seem to be pretty gung ho on getting what they want."

"What is that though?" she asked. "They're not saying anything."

"No, and it makes it that much harder to deal with them," Shelly said quietly. "I just keep hoping that something will happen, and we can get out of this nightmare."

"I don't know how," Mary said. "I didn't do anything."

"Neither did I," Shelly said.

"But at least you know somebody," she said resentfully. "That involves you more than it involves me."

Shelly stared at Mary in surprise. "It doesn't involve me at all, Mary. It's somebody I grew up with," she said. "And, as a matter of fact, he's putting his life in danger to come here."

"Well, if he's got a beef with these guys, it's best that they sort it out themselves and keep us out of it," Mary said, sounding bitter.

"Well, I'm not at all sure they have a beef with him," she said, and slowly she helped the older woman to sit down in a chair. The woman was shaky and distraught. Shelly understood where she was coming from, but it still didn't sit right that she would blame her or Shane. "Let's give the police a chance to sort this out," she said.

At that, Mary looked at her in surprise. "Do they even know?"

"Well, I would imagine so," she said, frowning. Then she stopped and winced. "It would be bad if they didn't."

"Of course it would," Mary said, "but it's bad no matter what. They came barging in here and killed the boss."

"And I don't understand that either," she murmured. "What's the point?"

"No resistance, I presume. He was the boss, and we all followed what he said. Take out the leader, and nobody knows what to do."

"Well, that's true enough to a certain extent." Shelly studied the older woman. "How many are at the office today?"

"Only twelve," she said. "I wanted to stay home, but I came in, not realizing what a mistake that would be."

"Have you not been feeling well?" Shelly asked the older woman.

Mary shook her head. "I haven't been feeling well for days," she said. "I'm just getting really tired and worn down."

"The office seems like it's been really stressful lately, hasn't it?"

"That's to put it mildly," Mary said. "Ever since Donnie quit, it's been pretty rough."

Donnie was the CFO, and he'd quit several weeks ago, under a cloud that had cast a pall over the company. "I wonder if he has anything to do with this."

"What would that have to do with your friend? Does he even know Donnie?"

"No, I don't think so," she said, quickly dismissing the idea. It was something she would love to pull out and pin on him, but it really would have nothing to do with Shane.

"What does your friend do?"

"He was in the navy," she said.

At that, Mary frowned. "What do they want him for then?"

"I have no idea," she said. She sat back and yawned. "It's really hard to just sit here and wait too."

"Well, the rest of us were all sitting out there in the one room," she said. "That's not exactly a picnic either."

Shelly smiled gently. "I know, and I'm sorry. I don't

know what's going on, but I can only hope it's all over with soon."

"Ha," Mary said. "I'm not sure we'll ever get out of this." She wrapped her arms around her chest and rocked herself gently on the chair.

"Have faith," she said.

"What kind of faith?" Mary said suspiciously. "I used to go to church all the time," she said, "until I lost that bit of faith too."

"I'm sorry," she said. "It sounds like you're a lost soul right now."

"I just wanted to go home, put my feet up, and visit with my cats!" she said.

"It's been a tough adjustment since your husband died, hasn't it?"

"Well, first my father, then my mother, and then my husband," she said, "and all within eighteen months."

At that, Shelly winced. "I'm so sorry. That's got to be brutal."

"It is. All I'd like to do now is go with them, but I can't trust anybody to look after my cats."

Shelly thought about that for a long moment. Is that all there was to life? To worry about who would look after your cats? Then again, she was a pet lover herself, and cats would be nice, especially now that she had a stable job. She almost snorted at that though, because she didn't have a stable job at all. The way things were going, she probably wouldn't have a job left by the time she got out of here. It was hard to say what kind of job she would end up with now. She shook her head, trying to clear it, but sleep and fatigue took over.

"Are you okay?" Mary asked.

"Yeah, just really supertired," she said. "Nothing like

being held hostage to raise you up and then drop you on the other side. I'm crashing, probably due to the adrenaline. I could really use a coffee."

"Well, I need to use the bathroom," Mary said, "but I'm not looking forward to asking for that either."

"Not only that," Shelly said, "they were here with me for a long time, and then they got up and left." She checked the clock up on the wall. "It's almost time."

"Time for what?"

"For my friend to arrive. They said forty minutes at first, but he was still stuck at the airport."

"You can't get anywhere in forty minutes if you're still at the airport," she said. "Have you seen the traffic there lately?"

"I know," she said. "So Shane said no way, but that he'd be here in two hours, and we're coming up on that. So I suspect that, when they come back here again, it'll be to haul me out."

"Oh, my gosh, aren't you terrified?"

"I don't know about terrified," she admitted, trying to hide how nervous she really was inside, "but I'm certainly not looking forward to this next step of whatever nightmare is going on here."

"No," Mary said, "me either. I just want to go home."

Just then the door opened. Both women were momentarily startled and stared at the man who stood there. It was the one they had called Joe. He looked at Mary, then looked at Shelly and pointed. "You, come on."

She hopped to her feet and said, "Mary here has to go to the bathroom," she murmured.

He looked at Mary, then shrugged and said, "That's nice."

"Well, it won't be nice if there's an accident," Shelly said. "The least you can do is take her to the washroom." He hesitated for a moment. She shrugged and said, "I'll sit here and wait."

He looked at Mary and said, "You have to go, huh?"

She immediately nodded. "Yes, please."

He nodded. "Come on then. You first."

Then Mary stood, shot Shelly a grateful look, and said, "Thank you."

At that, the older man sighed and said, "Hurry up. Let's go."

Mary moved out the door ahead of him, and the door swung shut immediately, leaving Shelly all alone.

GEARED UP IN a pair of overalls, Shane was already down in the sewer tunnels, standing just underneath the office building. "What the hell are we doing from here?" He studied the great big circular doorways that connected sewer tunnel to sewer tunnel, wondering how he was supposed to get through this next one because it wasn't opening. He had C-4 in his backpack but didn't want to take the chance of alerting any kidnapper that somebody was in the tunnels. He pulled his phone out and sent Gavin a message. **Can't open the last door.**

Give it a minute. We're working with the city right now.

He groaned and looked at Diesel. "They're working on it, but we're running out of time."

Diesel nodded. "Maybe it's just stuck. There's two of us," he said, "let's give it a try. See if we can put our weight together and get this done. Otherwise we'll have to blast the damn thing open because the kidnappers are expecting us at any moment."

"I know," Shane replied. With the two of them on the wheel, they worked at it until it finally gave. With that seal snapped open, they pushed their way into the center area of the telecom building. After that, they climbed up one level into a basement that let them into the utility area of the huge office building above. They quickly stripped down out of their protective gear and stashed it out of sight, then got their weapons ready and headed for the stairs. They had a map of the building and hoped to get up as high as they could undetected.

"You sure you want to trust that she's on the seventh floor?"

"Yes," he said. "We both attended Smithville for only the seventh grade. That is one thing I do trust."

"Okay," he said, "but you're putting an awful lot on her memory."

"No. She's just the kind of person who would think of something like that," he said. "Besides, we need something to go by, so I'll go by that." Diesel frowned but didn't say anything. Shane understood his hesitancy. Diesel didn't know Shelly the way Shane did. By the time they neared the fifth floor, there had been no sign of anyone. "Did the police clear out the rest of the building?" Shane asked.

"They did."

"Great," he said. "I want to go as far as the sixth, then take the elevator up."

"And what will you do when that door opens?"

"Well, I won't be there," he said, and he walked to the bank of elevators and quickly set each one for the seventh floor. When all six were on the way, he moved down the hall to the service elevator and from there he headed up to the seventh floor, on his own with Diesel. As soon as it opened, they came out with guns front and ready. But nobody was there. Frowning, he moved to the next hallway.

It was a huge building that looked to have at least forty different offices up here, and they were on the far side. At least they were on the same floor now as Shelly, but they had to get into the room where Shelly was held. As soon as they headed down one of the hallways, they knew they were going the right direction when they came across two bodies in the hallway—men who had been shot and killed for probably no other reason than the fact that they were heading for the elevator.

Shane took a photo, sent it to Gavin, shook his head, and kept on going. With semiautomatic rifles in hand, they moved slowly from hallway to hallway.

"What are you thinking about how best to get into the actual office?" Diesel whispered.

"Well, they'll let us in if we show ourselves," he said, "but there is another service elevator. I'd like to go up one floor and then come down."

"Which means that you'll be very late."

"Maybe, unless Gavin's doing his job."

"I guess it depends on if they can get a hold of him, huh?" Diesel said.

"Well, the kidnappers will be waiting because it's me they want after all." Finding another service elevator, he and Diesel quickly hopped up one floor and, once on the eighth floor, headed to the spot where Shane figured they'd been standing, just one floor below. "Now we have the offices at this end of the building," he said. "So what we need is that schematic to show us just which area we can go through into the washroom." Once they got a look, they realized the plumbing was stacked from floor to floor. "That's convenient."

"Well, it is for the plumbers," Diesel said. "It's also normal construction."

They quickly made their way into the bathroom, and, looking at the floor and the ceiling, Shane said, "Let's get through the vents." They quickly cut open one of the walls and found one of the big metal HVAC ducts. But they would have to cut into that as well. And that wouldn't be quite so easy. They had brought the tools, but it would take time.

When they finished that and had moved inside the men's bathroom, one floor below, their target floor, they had used up all the free time they could possibly have. They looked at each other and left the semiautomatics behind, stashed in the vents they came out of. With just handguns, they stepped out of the restroom into the hallway. With Diesel going left, Shane took a right. Just as he headed around the corner, he heard a woman speaking.

"She didn't say anything."

"Of course she didn't," he said. "At least we tried."

"Can I go back now?"

"Yeah. The boss wants to talk to you. I think he's ready to let you go home."

"Oh, yes, please," she said. "It's wasn't exactly a comfortable position, turning on somebody like that."

"You didn't say anything though," he said, "so your cooperation is appreciated." At that, he pointed to an office door and said, "The boss is in there."

As she headed to go in the wide-open door, Shane heard

a sharp burst and knew exactly how she'd been thanked. He groaned silently and closed his eyes, wondering what had happened and why that woman had been taken out. As the killer came around the corner, Shane whistled, didn't even give him a chance to react, and was on him in a second.

With a wicked uppercut, he snapped the guy's head back, then pummeled him in the torso and dropped him to the floor. He quickly dragged him into the room where he'd shot the poor woman. And he stopped and took a look. Snatching up his phone, he quickly took several photographs and sent them off. Nine dead people were in front, and a slighter woman was underneath a couple men in the back. He sent a message to Gavin. **Looks like they've been killing everyone.**

He sent the photo off to Diesel as well. As he stepped back out into the hallway, he sent another message to his partner. **One down.**

He got a message back from Diesel.

That makes two.

Shane grinned. Now that's what he liked, somebody who could keep track and count as they went. Because, dammit, no way in hell Shane wanted these killers to walk out of this building. He didn't know what the hell this was all about, but it was BS. As soon as he moved down the hallway toward the last area to be checked, he stopped and searched the small rooms to the side. Nobody was here. And why the hell was that? Had they killed everybody up here? He frowned at that. Maybe Shelly was already dead. He could hardly bear the thought, but, if that were the case, nobody was leaving this place until he'd taken them all out. She hadn't done anything to hurt anybody. Just then he heard a voice.

"Hello?"

He stepped forward and stuck his head around the next doorway.

Her eyes opened wide, and she looked at him. "Oh, my God," she said. "Shane?"

He grinned, opened his arms, and she bolted toward him. She was a lightweight, but she raced like a tornado and slammed him back against the wall. He hugged her close.

"Jesus!" she said. "I was hoping you'd come, but, at the same time, I was hoping you wouldn't."

He squeezed her tighter and asked, "Where are they?"

"I don't know," she said. "They came to get me, and then I convinced them to take Mary to the bathroom first because she needed to go. He said he'd be right back."

"Yeah, they took Mary to the bathroom all right," he said, "and then shot her in the head."

She stared at him, wordless, and then her jaw dropped. "Please, no," she said. "All she wanted to do was go home and rest."

"They convinced her to get some information out of you," he said, "which probably kept her alive a few minutes longer. When she came out of the bathroom, he sent her into a room, supposedly to talk to their boss before they let her go," he said. "Then he shot her while her back was turned."

She sagged against him. "I don't know what's going on," she whispered, "but these guys are assholes."

"You got that right," he said. "Let's get you out of here."

"How though?" she said. "There's no place to go."

He quickly pulled her back down and around in the direction that he'd come, moving as fast as they could. He sent Diesel a message that they were headed back to the men's bathroom. Shane kept checking, but he found nobody around. "Did you see the gunmen leave?"

"No," she said. "I don't know why they would. I'm wondering if they are in my boss's office."

"Where's that?"

"The other way," she said.

"Did they sound like they were waiting for somebody?"

"You," she said. "But, other than that, I don't know."

"Were they upset about the time frame?" he asked.

"Not really. They just snorted and said something like, it figured you wouldn't make it on time."

"Yeah, whatever," he said. By the time he got her into the bathroom, Diesel was already there.

He smiled. "Nice to meet you, ma'am."

She looked at him, and her eyes widened. "Wow," she said. "I don't know where you're from, but they sure build 'em big."

Diesel's face flushed, and he nodded and said, "That they do." Recovering quickly, he added, "Apparently you're from the opposite side of the country, where they make the women small."

She laughed in delight. "Yeah, I've never had much hope of getting any bigger either," she said. "My mom was under five feet tall. So, when I hit that, I figured I was doing well." She looked around and said, "How the hell do we get out of here?"

"I'm not sure," Diesel said, as he pointed to the way they'd come in. Smoke was coming through the hole.

Shane looked at the smoke and swore. "Is that coming from downstairs?"

"Yeah, I think they're a floor down, and they're trying to smoke us out," he said.

"In that case, we're going up," he said. "I found a room

with nine dead, including Mary, who'd been sitting with Shelly. Plus those other two dead we saw by the elevators."

"Eleven. Which means everybody but me," she said quietly. "At least in our department. How about everybody below us?"

"They were all cleared out," Shane said.

She shook her head. "So the bad guys have taken over the floor below? And how the hell are we supposed to leave?"

"Damn," he said, pointing at the smoke coming out from the vent, and looked at Diesel. "So only one way to go, right?"

"Looks like it," he said, and the two of them assessed the dangers of that. "You get the feeling we're getting pushed in one direction?"

"Absolutely," he replied.

"That's a danger in itself. Suggestions?"

"Not necessarily," he said. "We're short on options."

She frowned. "Well, I for one would much rather go down than up," she said.

"You and me both," he replied, walking to the vent. But he noted a sickening chemical odor to the smoke. "We can't get in there."

"So somewhere else maybe?" Shelly asked.

"Maybe," he said. He walked to the door and opened it, then looked out into the hallway. He stared at the glass on the other side and said, "We didn't come with rappelling equipment." She gasped at that. He turned, looked at her, then smiled reassuringly. "Obviously we wouldn't climb down the building unless it was safe."

"So do you think the entire floor down there is smoky?"

He nodded.

"Do you have more masks?"

"Nope, just the two. She frowned at that, her hands balled into fists, and said, "Well, that wasn't very forward thinking."

He just rolled his eyes at her. "We could only carry so much through the tunnels and still get up here."

"I suppose. But why can't we just go back down through that smoke?"

"Because a chemical agent has been added to it, possibly some drugs to knock us out," he said. "As a matter of fact, I'm not sure we can stay in here much longer." He pulled her forward into the hallway.

She stared at him in shock. "How about we go up, and you get a helicopter to take us off?"

"How about we go up, and they have a helicopter and a gunman waiting for us?"

She sucked in her breath and stared at him in shock. "Is that what they'll do?"

"That's what I would do," he said. He glanced back at the gas coming up from the open vent. "Is that dissipating at all?"

"It is," Diesel replied. "If one of us puts wet cloths over our faces, we might get down a flight or two."

"Well, that would be better than up at this point," he said. "But the thing is, we have to get past the next floor and at least get down to the fifth."

"I think we can do that," Diesel said. Suddenly they heard some noises. Shane looked at Diesel, who said, "It appears we don't have any choice."

Shane took his mask and put it on Shelly, despite her objections. "Not now, Shelly."

Diesel put his on. They quickly grabbed wads of paper towels and soaked them in the men's room sink. Then Shane took off his shirt and wrapped it around his nose and mouth, tying it tight in the back. "Close your mouth," he told Shelly, and then he put the wet paper towels inside the mask up against her mouth. He and Diesel did the same with the rest of the wet paper towels. Next thing she knew, she was picked up with a shriek.

"Don't," Shane said. "Not a word. Now keep your eyes closed and hang on tight."

She sucked in her breath and held on to him. She didn't know what was going on but assumed they were going inside the ventilation shaft. She burrowed close against his neck, worried that he didn't have a mask on. The next thing she knew, they were inside and slowly working their way down. She didn't know if he was trying to cough, but he wasn't breathing very much.

Suddenly they burst through the bottom of a vent and went down even farther. When he came out the other side, he put her down, then rolled onto the ground, hacking and coughing.

She quickly pulled the shirt off his face and looked at him. "Oh, my God. Shane, are you okay?"

He nodded, but his eyes were streaming. She handed the wet paper towels from her mask to him, as he immediately put them on his eyes. She checked on Diesel. She and Diesel made it through better, with the masks. "You guys could have been killed doing that," she said crossly.

Diesel laughed. "Well, we could have been," he said, "but chances were good that we wouldn't." He looked at Shane, who had stopped coughing now.

"Now," Shane rasped, "let's get you out of here." He coughed one more time, and his eyes seemed to be better.

"Sure," she said. "You got any idea how?"

"Well, we could take the stairs," he said, "but the elevator might be faster." He quickly grabbed her hand and raced her to the elevator. "I wish there was a whole bank of them," he said, as he pushed the buttons. One opened almost immediately, and he pulled her inside, and Diesel stepped in right behind them.

"Will they be waiting for us?"

"Well, let's hope not," he said, "but we're ready for them just in case."

She shook her head. "How can you take all this so lightly?" she murmured. But she was studying Diesel too, and he appeared to be taking it all in stride, the same as Shane. "Is this the life you lead too?" she asked him.

He looked at her, smiled, and said, "Well, I retired a while ago," he said, "but it doesn't appear to be sticking."

She shook her head. "Jesus, if this is your idea of retirement—"

The door opened just then, and nobody appeared to be outside waiting for them. The men stepped out carefully, but the wide corridor was empty. She was walked down the hallway—past where the security staff should have been—which led outside. Immediately they were surrounded by first responders and separated. She cried out for Shane, only to see him surrounded by armed SWAT. She was rushed off to an ambulance, where she was checked over. The oxygen really helped, but she tried to tell the EMT that Shane really needed oxygen. When the EMT failed to listen, she finally shouted at him.

"Those two men saved me," she snapped. "They need oxygen.

The EMT looked at her in surprise, then looked to where Shane and Diesel still stood, surrounded by SWAT and NYPD, but with their hands in the air. The EMT walked over and immediately put an oxygen mask on each of them. When the cops surrounding them tried to argue, the EMT shook his head and pointed at her.

One of the cops came over and asked Shelly, "What can you tell us about this?"

CHAPTER 3

"**S**HANE'S THE GUY the terrorists were waiting for," she said. "He's like special ops or something. Shane and his partner came in, rescued me, and brought me out." He looked at her in shock, then raced back to the others. It took another few minutes to get the all clear, and, apparently by then, everybody had calmed down. She sagged against the side of the ambulance. One of the ambulance drivers was a woman.

She looked at Shelly and said, "Exciting day for you."

"Not by choice," she said. "I'd have been happy to stay home with a cup of coffee and miss all this."

"Yeah. Some days are like that, aren't they?"

"Yeah, I guess," she said, yawning. "Gosh, I'm really sleepy all of a sudden."

"Stress will do that do you. Do you want to jump in here and lie down on the gurney?"

She looked up at her gratefully and said, "I would love to, but I don't need to go to the hospital or anything."

"Come on. Just go ahead and lie down for a few minutes," she said. "It's not a problem. Here. I can shut the door and give you some peace and quiet."

Maybe it was what she'd just been through, or maybe it was everything else going on in her world, but Shelly just wasn't feeling it. "No, that's okay. Thanks, though." And, with that, she hopped off and walked to where Shane stood, still explaining what had gone on. She caught the relief in his face when he saw her. She walked over, wrapped her arms around him, and just held on tight. "I don't want to let you go," she said.

"Ditto." He held her close, as he answered all the questions.

She turned and looked at the uniformed officers. "Did you guys even go up there? Did you go in and start a recovery mission?" she snapped. "Did you get to the roof to see how the killers are getting out of here?"

"There's been no sign of anybody leaving the building," Shane answered before anyone could. "I told Gavin that we had left, and they already had people looking through the same tunnels we used to get in. So far, nobody's been there, according to the cameras."

"So they're still in the building then," she said, staring up at him.

"That's what they're organizing now," he said, with a nod to the authorities. "A complete sweep of the building."

"Well, make sure they stop at the seventh floor," she said sadly, turning to the cops. "That's where all my dead coworkers are." She looked up at Shane. "Thank you for saving my life, by the way."

"You're welcome," he said, as he dropped a tender kiss on her forehead and just cuddled her close.

"Life sucks sometimes. I was really enjoying that job, and my coworkers were great. How could these men do that to them?"

"The men couldn't risk leaving anyone alive. There might be a job here still," he said.

She snorted. "I think everybody was killed."

"Just in your department," he said.

"I'll never walk back into that office. Or this building," she announced.

"I hear you, but that doesn't mean you have to give up on everything."

"No," she smiled, "not everything. Just this part."

He squeezed her gently. "Sorry, honey."

"I'm not," she said. "There are things in life to worry about, but that's not one of them."

He chuckled and said, "Trust you to be very pragmatic about it all."

She shrugged. "What else can I do?" She said, "It is what it is." She looked up at Diesel. "Thanks for getting conned into helping him out."

He laughed. "What makes you think I was conned into it?"

"You mean, you weren't?"

He just smiled and nodded. "Shane and I go back a long time."

"Wow, and you still came when he called. You must be one who makes good friends."

"I too make good friends," Shane said, with a smile. "After all, you're my friend."

"That's true," she said, returning his smile. She looked around at the cops all milling around. "Are we able to leave now?"

"I hope so," Shane said. "I missed lunch."

At that, she started the laugh, but very quickly the laughter turned to tears.

He hugged her tight and told the cops standing there, "I'm taking her back to the hotel. She needs a chance to recuperate in a safe, quiet place for a little bit." The cops nodded and, returning their weapons to them, let them leave.

As they walked away, she asked, "How many guns were you carrying anyway?"

"Oh, a couple more than they took off me," he said, with that special smile of his. "All completely legit by the way," he added, in a mild tone of voice.

"Unbelievable," she said. "You actually got permission? That doesn't sound like you."

"Hey," he said, "I have a new job. I get to be a little bit of a rogue now and then."

"Now and then? That's amazing," she said. "Does that mean you can get me out of here? I'm ready to go home."

"Well, we'll go to the hotel, not to your place."

"Why not?" she asked. "I want to get a shower, change clothes, then find that bottle of wine in my fridge, so I don't have to think about Mary and the rest of the people from my office."

"Well, we can arrange the shower at the hotel, but I don't know about the change of clothing," he said. "That's the information I gave the cops, so we need to be there."

"*You* need to be there," she said. "I don't. I can go back to my place."

He just glared at her, until she raised her hands in frustration, then surrender.

"Seriously? Fine," she said. "Can we at least run past my place, so I can pack an overnight bag?"

"We can do that," he said. "We'll grab a cab." She groaned, and they quickly hailed one. She gave him her address, and they headed off to her place. As she sagged in the front seat and stayed quiet, the cab driver looked at her.

"Bad day?"

"The worst," she replied. When he pulled up in front of her place, Shane paid him and said, "Can you wait here for a few minutes? We'll be heading to a hotel." The cab driver agreed and put the light on, and they quickly headed up to her apartment.

As she walked through the apartment, Diesel asked, "How long have you been here?"

She followed his gaze to the stacks of boxes in the corner. "Obviously not long enough to unpack yet," she said. "Six weeks."

"Wow," he said. "Will you stay?"

"I don't think so," she said. "As much as I enjoyed the job, I really missed California. New York is such a massive city, and yet, well, I always feel alone."

"Seems like a good time for a move," Shane said.

"That's what this move to New York was about," she said. "I guess I didn't tell you about that, but I was just tired of the same old thing all the time." As she walked into her master bedroom, she passed a pile of unpacked boxes there as well. Shaking her head, she grabbed her overnight bag and quickly packed a few outfits. She looked around to see the guys checking out every nook and cranny in the apartment and said, "I haven't even had a chance to really move in," she said, "let alone get settled." She looked up at the two men, then smiled and said, "Come on. Let's get out of here. Otherwise I'll want to shower and get changed right here. If I do, you'll probably have to pack me out of here on your shoulder."

"Okay, but Diesel's packing you this time," Shane said with a chuckle. "Let's go," he murmured, slinging an arm around her neck.

"You're sure I can't just get a quick shower here?" She

tried again, looking around the small apartment that still didn't feel like home.

"Nope, sorry," he said. "Let's go."

She groaned and let herself be led out of her apartment. Back outside, they headed to the cab. They got in, and Diesel gave the driver the hotel address. As they headed out, she twisted around and said to Shane, "How long do we have to stay at the hotel?"

"I don't know," he said, "but at least tonight."

She shrugged and said, "Fine. That won't kill me." She sighed, settled back, and wondered at the direction they were going. As she turned to double-check with Shane, it occurred to her the driver seemed bigger than she remembered. Just as she started to speak, the window between the front and back seat abruptly closed, and all the locks snapped shut. She twisted to look at the cab driver. "Seriously?"

He looked at her and said, "Just sit there and be quiet."

"After what I've been through today," she said, her temper getting the best of her, "the hell I will." She reached out and smacked him hard across the face.

Immediately he pulled the handgun from his waist and held it up against her face. "I said, sit down and shut up."

She glared at him. "Fine. I'll sit," she snapped. "But, Jesus, this is really not the time to piss me off."

"Shut up!" he roared.

"What do you think will stop these guys from taking you out?"

"It's bulletproof glass," he said. "Now sit there and *shut up*. I'm not telling you again." She turned and stared forward, but inside she was fuming and terrified. "What's this all about?"

"You got out of the office building," he said, trying to

steer while talking to her and managing the handgun, "and I was asked to replace the other cab with my own," he said. "I often do special trips for people."

"What? You just happened to be handy?"

"Actually I was on call, like a backup."

"That's nice," she said snidely.

As they came up to a red light, he looked like he would slow down to take a turn.

Immediately she grabbed the wheel and yanked on it hard. The vehicle spun around in the middle of the intersection, and she started hitting him with all her might. Because she was half climbing all over him, he couldn't get the gun in position to hurt her. He reached up to grab her by the neck, but, before he had a chance, she punched the lock button, unlocking the doors. Then she punched him as hard as she could in the face.

Blood spurted from his nose, and she tried to jerk back from his grip, now pinching the upper part of her arm. Just as he got his other arm free, the driver's side door popped open, and, in no time, Diesel and Shane had pulled him out and tossed him to the ground in the middle of the intersection. Immediately the gun flung free, and the man scrambled after it. Shane punched him once and then again, and the gunman went down in a heap. Shane walked over and kicked the gun away from his body and stood over him, pulling out his phone.

She had no clue what was going on, but she admired his technique. She would have to work on hers.

Shane glared at her from outside the cab. "What the hell

did you think you were doing?"

"Improvising," she said, with a shrug. Diesel laughed. She looked at him and said, "At least one of you has a sense of humor."

"Well," Diesel said, "if you were mine, I'd have turned you over my knee and gave you a spanking."

She looked at him, shocked. "Damn good thing I'm not then," she said in an ominous tone, "because anybody who thinks that's a good idea won't do well with me."

"I was kidding," Diesel said, "but you had to know Shane would be unhappy about what you just did."

"Why?" she said. "At least we're not all locked inside a damn taxi right now, being taken to God-only-knows where," she said. "In case nobody noticed, I'm a little tired of being ordered around today."

"Got it," he said, with a smile, and she glared at him suspiciously. He just turned and motioned toward Shane, who stood there still glaring at her, his hands on his hips.

She hopped out of the cab and immediately put her hands on her own hips, imitating his posture perfectly. "Come on. You know I won't be the one who sits there and follows orders," she complained.

Rolling his eyes, Shane pinched the bridge of his nose. "You could at least try *not* to get yourself killed."

"Well, obviously you guys wouldn't be any help," she said. "What was I supposed to do?"

He stared at her, shaking his head. "You never change, do you?"

"Am I supposed to?" she asked, and he heard a little bit of insecurity in her voice. He sighed, then opened his arms, and she ran into them. He closed them around her immediately and held her tight. "You always got into trouble at every turn."

"I also get out of trouble, thank you very much," she said.

"You're also damned lucky sometimes."

"Well, obviously I picked a time when I knew his hands would be busy," she said. "You should be nice to me, since I did get us out of that ugly situation."

"Oh, yeah," he said, "I'm really happy about it. Now, do you think you can stay out of trouble long enough to let us check this guy over and make sure he doesn't pull something else?"

"Not to worry," Diesel said. "I just patted him down. No ID on him. Lots of cash in his back pocket, but, other than that, there's nothing."

"Anything in the cab?"

"No registration papers and the license plate doesn't belong on it either."

"Figures."

In the meantime, the cops finally arrived, as the traffic had slowly been going around them, but they were definitely a hazard. When they tried to explain what had happened, they just looked at him in shock. "What?"

Then she said, "We were the ones in that office-building-hostage thing that just happened," she added, the words all tumbling out.

Shane pulled her back into his arms, held her close, and said, "Just stay calm." Then he explained everything to the officer, who just shook his head.

"Jesus," he said, "can you guys just get to the hotel and stay out of trouble?"

"Maybe," she said, lifting her head away from Shane's chest. "Will you provide any security to keep us out of trouble? We took a cab. That's all we did. We took a cab to my place to pick up some clothes, and then we were supposed to go back to the hotel. That's it," she said. "So how the hell is that our fault?"

Shane squeezed her shoulders and said, "Sorry, guys. She's a little overwrought."

The officer looked at her like she was a time bomb. She just rolled her eyes. Shane glared at her and said, "Calm down, would you please?"

She sighed, then slumped against him and nodded. "Okay, this is your show," she said. "But you'll have to get me something to eat soon." She yawned and snuggled in close. He sighed and said, "Any chance you guys could give us a lift to the hotel? We stopped at her place to pick up a change of clothing, and the cab switched while we were inside. We said we'd be available to answer more questions, but we got held up." He then provided the name of the SWAT leader from the telecom building task force.

Nodding, the officer said, "Come on. Get in the back of my cruiser here." Shane led her to the police car, and the three of them piled into the back. She never said another word, until they were outside the hotel.

Looking up at the third-rate hotel, she smiled. "This is all you can afford, huh? I guess they don't pay you that well for those missions."

He just sighed, shaking his head. "We were trying to avoid calling any attention to ourselves. We're not trying to impress anyone or to make a statement with our lodging choices anyway."

She looked at him sideways. "Yeah, so how's that working out for you?" At that, Diesel laughed and laughed. She glared at him. "What's so funny now?"

"You two," he said. "You're really great together."

"We're not exactly *together*-together," she said.

"He knows that," Shane said. "He's probably figuring out why we aren't."

"Well, I probably irritate you way too much," she said. "And, in all honesty, I kind of irritate myself. So I'm not sure what to do about that."

"Well, you could just get along in life," Shane said. "You don't always have to be at the front of all the trouble."

"Wouldn't that be nice," she said, "if such a thing were even possible. But remember. I just came here to do a job. I didn't have anything to do with starting that mess at my office. That was all on you, buddy."

"I know," he said, "and I thank you very much for your assistance."

"Right," she said, hearing the overly patronizing tone in his voice. In no time, they make it up to their room. She sat down on one of the two queen beds in the room, then looked around and said, "We better not be here for the whole night," she said, "because there isn't room for all three of us."

"Yes, there is," Shane said. "One of us will always be on watch through the night."

"Oh, good," she said. "I really need to get some sleep first, but then I can take a watch."

"You'll get to sleep all night," Shane said. "We'll handle the watch."

"No, really. I'll take a watch."

"No."

She glared at him and then gave in. "Right. Now you'll say, 'This is what we do,' right?"

Diesel quietly chuckled at the way she dropped her voice

and changed her posture to imitate Shane.

"Do you really want to argue over this?" Shane asked her.

"No, I guess not," she said, "but seriously, can we get some food? I'm starving."

"Yes, we'll get some food," he said. "We'll order room service."

She wrinkled up her face at that. "Yeah, I can just imagine what the kitchen in this place looks like. I think there was a pizza place around the corner, maybe a steakhouse. Can we leave?"

"No."

"Steak from takeout would be cold and overcooked," she said, "but pizza on the other hand …" And she waggled her eyebrows. "Come on. We have a long history of sharing a pizza and talking all night."

"Yes, we do," he said. "Go get your shower, and we'll see what we can come up with." She grinned, then snagged her overnight bag and raced into the bathroom.

Diesel looked on, shaking his head. "Man, I don't know," he said. "I think the two of you are a perfect match."

"Hell no," he said. "You heard how it is. Trust me. We do much better *not* together."

"I'm not so sure about that," Diesel said. "I don't think you've ever given it a chance."

"Did you see her in that cab?" he said. "I damn near had a heart attack when she reached over and smacked him the first time, much less when she grabbed the steering wheel, jumped on top of him, punching him in the face."

"I did too," Diesel admitted. "Is she always that hot-tempered?"

"Yeah, but she's also very good-hearted. She would say

that she only loses it when people need it."

Diesel snorted at that. "She's something," he said. "When she snapped at that cop, I thought she might talk us right into handcuffs."

"I know it," he said, laughing at the memory. "Like I said, she's generally pretty good with it, but she's been under a lot of stress with this hostage deal."

"You think?" Diesel said. Then he added, "What's it gonna be? Pizza or steak?"

"Well, I was hoping for a damn steak," he said, "but she's right. Steak should be served sizzling hot, and we won't get that from takeout, and, now that she mentioned it, we might save ourselves a gut ache by skipping room service."

"So …"

"Pizza it is," he said. "We need to just find one nearby that delivers."

"No problem," Diesel said. "There's one across the street."

"Oh, good," he said, "one of us can just walk across and grab something, instead of delivery."

"Why don't I go over and take a look," he said.

"Would you mind?"

"Hell no," he said. "I'm just as damn tired and hungry as the two of you. I'll go get some food, and, maybe by the time I get back, you'll have both showered, so I can hop in."

"We'll make it happen," Shane said and smiled, as Diesel headed out.

CHAPTER 4

S HELLY STOOD UNDER the hot water, letting it sluice down her back, easing some of the knots of stress that had settled into her shoulders and the back of her neck. She wanted to stay here and not move again. She'd prefer a soak in a hot tub after a good steak and a glass of red wine, but, since those options weren't available, she better get moving. She stood there for a moment longer and scrubbed her hair.

She was in rough shape by the time she finished. She was tired from the heat, exhausted from the events of the day, and felt her energy waning. Finally she shut off the water, wrapped up in a towel, and just sat on the end of the bathtub for a few minutes. By the time she dried herself down, she felt a little better.

Just then came a knock on the door, and Shane called out, "You okay?"

"I'm fine," she said with a sigh. Moving quickly to her bag, she slipped on underclothes, then threw on an oversize T-shirt and a pair of leggings. As she opened the door, she finished brushing out her hair and said, "Sorry. I'm taking a long time."

"It's all good," he said, his gaze searching her face. "I'm just worried about you."

"I appreciate that," she said with a bright smile. "It's been a rough day."

"That's an understatement," he said with a nod. "Bet you never have to experience a workday like that again."

"Yeah," she said. "Not likely." Taking a deep breath, she continued, "The problem is that I saw at least four of them. And they all know who I am."

He nodded slowly. "I was wondering if you connected those dots."

She glared at him and said, "I know I'm not in your field and don't have experience with all this cloak-and-dagger stuff, but I do have a brain. Since they made a point of leaving no other witnesses alive, odds are they won't leave a loose end like me out here. Hence the cabbie."

"Unfortunately you're absolutely right," he said boldly.

She winced. "You could go ahead and sugarcoat it a little, you know?" she said with a groan. "You never have been one to mince words, have you?"

"You want me to lie to you?"

"Of course not," she said. Tossing the hairbrush into her bag, she gave the ends of her hair one last squeeze before hanging up the towel and stepping into the other room. "It's just so depressing," she said.

"We've not yet heard from the police or Gavin on how the building sweep went down or how badly the ones Diesel and I took down were hurt."

"You're right, thank you. We'll know more before long, I'm sure. Are we really staying here?"

"Well, I was contemplating another room, if that would make you feel better. We gave the fake cabbie this address, but he's in custody."

She immediately shook her head. "Oh no, I'm fine with all of us bunking in here, if you guys don't mind an extra houseguest."

"We're fine with it," he said and gently squeezed her shoulder. "You did really well in there today."

She looked up at him, and, in spite of herself, the tears came to her eyes again.

"Come here," he said and pulled her into his arms again.

"I was so scared," she said, "and, when they told me that they were after you, I just couldn't believe it."

He kissed her gently on the temple. "I'm sorry, I don't know what's behind all this because I haven't heard directly from any of them," he said. "But I will get to the bottom of it."

"I know you will," she said, and, with a sigh, she stepped back a bit, rotated her shoulders, and added, "That cabbie just pissed me off."

He snorted, remembering how tickled Diesel had gotten when they'd talked about it. "You think?" he said. "Not the smartest move."

"No, that was on him," she said, "trying to drive, while holding the gun on me. He'd have been better off if he'd gotten me to drive instead."

"That's very true," he said. "Which makes me think he wasn't used to doing something like this."

"Maybe I should feel happy about that," she said, "but I don't." He just smiled, and she glared at him. "Do you find this funny?"

"There is *nothing* funny about this at all," he said, with emphasis. "So, no, I don't find it funny."

"I know," she said. "Sorry. I'm just out of sorts."

"You're allowed to be," he murmured. "Nobody expects you to be perfect or to handle everything gracefully all the time."

She nodded, pulling her wet hair into a ponytail high on

the top of her head and said, "But you know? We get used to being *on* all the time. Used to handling everything and being perfect because it's required."

"None of that is ever required when you're with me."

"That's the thing about you," she said, with a bright smile. "I can just be me."

"I hope so," he said. "Don't ever think that's not enough."

"Yeah, yeah, yeah," she said, and then, with a cheeky grin, she added, "So did you order any food?"

"Diesel's gone to pick it up."

"Oh, gosh, but he's tired too," she said, feeling terrible for making a fuss about room service.

"A pizza joint's right across the street," he said. "It's not like he's running a marathon."

She relaxed at that. "Oh, good, I felt guilty about turning my nose up at room service," she said. "I really like him. He seems like a nice guy."

"He is." He looked at her. "And speaking of nice guys, what happened to that last boyfriend of yours?"

"*Ugh.* He got too possessive," she said. "We broke up months ago."

"I'm sorry."

"Yeah, yeah," she said. "I'll find the right guy one of these days."

"Or maybe you could just stop trying so hard and see who shows up."

"Well, I've tried that too," she said, "and nobody turned up." He burst out laughing, and she grinned at him. "Besides, you were out of town."

"Were you waiting for me?" he asked, shaking his head with a bright smile.

"Maybe," she said. "Did you ever think about what our life would be like if we were together?"

"No," he said, his tone joking, "I never did."

"See? Now I don't know," she said, "but I feel like that's just an insult."

He snorted at that and said, "We talked about it briefly once. I've known you for a very long time, and anything you've wanted in your life, you've gone after. Never, at any point in time, have you showed me that you were even remotely interested."

"That's not true," she protested. The she added, with good humor, "You know how much I love you."

"Loving me and being *in love* with me," he said, "are two different things.

"Sometimes I wonder though," she said. "I think we get so hung up on perfection—the perfect match for the perfect future—that we tend to forget a whole lot better things are out there than *perfect*."

He stopped her, and, looking puzzled, he asked, "Like what?"

She gave him a slow smile. "Like things that naturally fall into place with a sense of rightness."

"Doesn't that make it perfect?"

She shrugged. "But it seems like it's contrived otherwise. When we're always out there, looking for something better, we forget to see what's nearby because we're so hung up on the seeking. The pursuit for something outside that might be a better match, or I don't know," she said, shrugging. "Sorry. I'm not making any sense with my rambling. I didn't realize how tired I am."

"You're exhausted," he said, "but that doesn't mean you're not making sense."

She rolled her eyes at him and looked at the beds. "Do you care which bed I crash on?" He shook his head. She set her overnight bag on the bed closest to the bathroom and threw herself up against the headboard, piling all the pillows up, so she could curl up under a blanket.

"Don't you want to sleep?"

"Sure," she said, "but my stomach's growling, and I'm afraid that, every time I close my eyes, I'll see Mary. I still don't know what they were hoping she would get out of me."

"Probably information on me," he said.

"Maybe, but it's not like you ever tell me what you're doing," she said, "so I didn't know anything of value anyway."

"Maybe," he murmured. "Have we been that distant?"

"Nope, but I was never one to sit there and bug you as to where you were at any given moment in time, so why would it be any different when I haven't seen you for months?"

"Maybe they thought we were closer."

"That's because we text all the time," she said. "And that's great for staying in touch, but it doesn't really give you the nitty-gritty details of what's going on in somebody's life." She yawned. "I didn't have anything to tell her anyway. So it doesn't make a whole lot of difference," she added, exhaling a big breath, stretching out on the bed. "Did you say pizza was coming?"

He laughed. "He should be here any minute." At that came a knock on the door. He opened it up and let Diesel in, carrying three large boxes.

She stared, dumbfounded. "Wow," she said. "I know how much I eat, and I know how much Shane can eat, so you must be expecting to fill up on the rest of it."

Diesel laughed, then turn to Shelly. "Actually you might want to consider that we could be here for a while."

She winced at that. "Now that won't make me happy. I'd much rather go home."

"Maybe so," he said, "but that doesn't mean you'll be allowed to."

She stared at him, her gaze going from Diesel to Shane and back. "Why wouldn't I be allowed to go home?"

"For the same reason that you already thought of," Shane said quietly, walking to sit down beside her. She stared at him, not understanding. He winced. "Remember our conversation about them still being after you?"

"Speaking of which, how would they know who I am or where I live? How did the fake cabbie know to go there?"

"The gunmen in the tower knew who you were before the cabbie got there. Were you separated from your purse at any time while they held you?"

She sucked in her breath and frowned. "Yes."

"So that's one way they could have gotten your address, if they didn't have it already. They also could have accessed your employment records while they were there," he said. "Or they could have been watching for a few days. Trust me. They knew long before. And you already know that they are concerned about witnesses. Otherwise there was no reason for the cabbie switch."

"But you were there. Do you really think I'm in danger with you around?"

"Until we have a better idea of who these people are and why they used you to get to me," he said, "I think we have to continue to be as careful as we can."

She got up and walked to the three boxes that Diesel had

opened up. Taking one look, she smiled broadly, and, since there were no plates, she ripped the top off one of the boxes, then folded it, so she had a good thick piece of cardboard. Arranging a few pieces on it, she sat down in the nearest chair. The men followed suit, minus the cardboard. By the time she had eaten two pieces, she had mentally worked through the problem. "That's why you didn't want me to stay at my place or even take time to shower, isn't it?"

"I'm pretty sure they already knew exactly where you lived," he said, "and that's how they were able to get that cab in place so quickly."

Understanding crossed her features, as she remembered the scene with the taxi driver. "Great, so how do we solve this?"

"That's the question," Shane said, "and we're waiting on intel."

"Intel from whom?" she asked. He looked up to see her eyeing him sharply. "Exactly who do you work for?"

"A black ops program," he said. "Yes, it's with the government. It's secret and includes all that good spy stuff, but, just like everybody else in the world, we have to come up with information that's usable."

"Well, let's hope we get some fast," she said. "I may not have been terribly impressed with my life here, but that doesn't mean I was ready to have it completely stopped."

"Oh, it stopped, make no mistake about that," he said, his voice hard. "Your boss is gone, along with your whole department. The company will have to do a massive reassessment, and you need to be prepared to have people hold you responsible in some way."

"What?" She stared at him in shock. "But I didn't do anything."

"You did though. You survived," he said quietly. "You know people are like that."

She shook her head. "But that's like victimizing me all over again."

"I know, but I don't think the company will give a damn," he said. "They'll show you sympathy, but, at the same time, you'll be a bit of a pariah nobody'll want anything to do with."

She groaned. "I don't think I like human nature much."

"That's the thing. It doesn't matter if you like it or not," Diesel said, with a note of amusement. "We still have to live in this world."

"So what am I supposed to do?"

"First, you'll sit here and relax," Shane said. "Second, as soon as I've eaten, I'll see if any information has come in. And then we need a game plan."

"Like, for me to go away for a holiday?" she said. "I like that idea."

He gave a grunt of amusement. "Aren't you funny," he said. "The reality is, you may just have to go into hiding, until we can solve this thing."

Her eyes widened. "And how long would that be?" she asked, an ominous edge to her voice.

He looked at her, then winced and said, "It could be a matter of weeks."

"Oh, hell, no," she said. "Because, when you say weeks, what you actually mean is that it could be months, and no way I can put my life on hold like that."

"And I get that," he said, trying to forestall her arguments.

"No," she said, "you don't get it at all. It's just not something I can do."

"It is something you *can* do," he corrected gently. "It's not something you would *choose* to do, and that's the big difference."

She groaned and stared at him. "How about you've got one week?" she asked. "You're the one always telling me about your can-do attitude, so you've got one week to solve this."

"And then what?" he asked.

Diesel watched the exchange in fascination.

She just glared at Shane. "You solve this, and then you help me figure out what I'm doing for a job now. How will I ever fill out an application or go on a job interview? *Reason for termination? Entire department annihilated by terrorists,*" she said sarcastically.

"You'll find another job," Shane said. "You've never had any problem finding work before."

"No, but I've never been targeted by terrorists before either."

"I'm not sure we'll call them terrorists," he said. "But, with this many deaths, you know there'll be an awful lot of police on the case."

"Perfect, so let them solve it." Then she glared at him and said, "But you won't let them solve it, will you?"

"Of course not," he said, with a bright smile. "And, if you're being honest, you don't want me to let them do it either. You want me to get out there and to solve it right now, so you can get your life back."

Her shoulders slumped, and she nodded. "And it won't happen, will it?"

"It will happen," he said, "but I don't know when or what life will look like in the meantime. We have to be adaptable, but, most important, we have to make sure that the three of us are safe."

She nodded slowly. "Because they were really after you. Why though? What did they want you for?"

"Well, it would have been nice to find that out," he said. "With any luck the taxi guy might tell us something."

"Maybe," she said, staring out the window. "But it feels like it must have been a huge game plan, and they went to a lot of effort to get to you." She turned to look at him and asked, "What have you done, or who have you done something to that could bring all this on?"

He shook his head. "I've been involved in dozens of missions all over the world," he said quietly. "If somebody wanted to hold me personally responsible, they certainly could, but I would be no more personally responsible than all the other men involved in the same operation."

"So that's the question then, isn't it?" she said, staring at him. "Have any of your other black-ops friends gone missing?"

SHANE WASN'T EVEN sure where that thought had come from, but he stared at Shelly in surprise, then turned to look at Diesel.

Diesel shrugged. "She's got a point. But, if somebody had taken out a whole team, we might not even know—because we've been out of service for a while." He turned to look back at her, still frowning.

She shrugged. "It sounds like something you need to consider," she said. "Like, maybe you're the last resort. Particularly if you're not part of an active naval unit anymore. For all you know, there has been a major accident, and a unit was taken out, and you were the last one on the list. Or, hell, maybe they're even starting with you. But, if you overthrew a government, put somebody behind bars, got somebody kicked out of the navy—who the hell knows what it may have been—but revenge can take a long time to develop, as people make plans to get even."

"I wouldn't even know where to start to look for something like that," Shane said quietly.

"With your old superiors," she said, "I would think. I don't know how many people you've actually dealt with or how it all works, which puts me at a disadvantage on crafting a solution."

"Not to mention the fact that I'm no longer in the navy anymore," he said, with half a smile.

"I get that," she said. "You've left the navy but not the government. But that doesn't mean these killers know that, or perhaps the very act of leaving the navy is what opened it up so they could get to you."

He shook his head. "Now you're reaching a bit."

"And you're ignoring an obvious question that needs to be asked."

"She's right," Diesel said, and there was such a surprise in his voice that she turned on him, an eyebrow raised.

Shane laughed. "She's often right," he said. "She has a very different mind-set."

"I do not," she said crossly.

"Do so," he said, with affection. She just glared at him, and he laughed.

"Like I said," Diesel said, "you two make a great couple."

"It would never work," she said, shaking her head.

"Why is that?" Diesel asked, studying her carefully.

"I'm all about monogamy, and he wants to play the field."

"That's not true," Shane protested.

She looked at him in surprise. "Since when?"

"I haven't 'played the field,' as you call it, for at least four or five years," he said.

Her eyebrows shot up. "Seriously?"

"Yeah," he said, "it was a stage. I was happy to not settle down and to just enjoy life, and so were you, as I recall."

"Sure, but I am much more interested in relationships that don't have a start and an end date," she said.

He burst out laughing at that. "You apparently haven't updated your information on me lately."

"Obviously I didn't realize you'd finally gotten to the point of wanting to settle down. I figured you were still up for traveling the world, being wild and crazy."

"Traveling the world is never a bad thing," he said. "Besides, you don't know what you'll do now. Maybe you'll end up doing more traveling."

"Maybe," she said, "I was actually thinking about it, but I don't really know. Right now, it's hard to know anything. Except one thing. ... I don't really want to go back into tall New York City office buildings."

"Like the ones with seven floors?"

"Especially not the ones with seven floors," she said. "Although I'm not too thrilled with the idea of being in buildings that have more than two. Actually I'd like to stay on the ground floor for now."

"It's amazing how an incident like that can really affect you. It makes sense though," he said. "When you think about it, your life has not always been the easiest, and, when you go through something traumatic like that, it's hard to get past it."

"I don't want it to be the thing that I remember about my entire life though," she said. "That would be terrible. There's got to be so much more in my world than to survive being held by terrorists—or whatever you want to call that attack."

"Well, it was definitely a targeted assault," he said, "but I'm not sure it was for men and country."

"Well, I don't know what else it was, but they said that I was a means to an end to get you here," she said. She glared at him. "Do you know what that felt like? To know that all they were doing was waiting for you to show up, and that I was responsible for getting you there?"

"Hey, I came here of my own free will," he said in a mild tone, knowing perfectly well that she would take that guilt on no matter what he said. "You are not responsible. These guys were. Besides," he added, "did you ever get a chance to take a picture of any of the kidnappers?"

She shook her head. "No. Our phones were taken away. Just like our purses, and we even had to empty our pockets. Everything that we had on us was taken away."

"Would you recognize them again?"

"Of course," she said. "Why?"

"Could you give a police artist information for a sketch?"

She stopped and stared at him. "I don't know," she said. "I didn't see the one hardly at all, but the other two were all in black. The only one I really saw close must have been one of the two guys you and Diesel took out."

"Interesting," he murmured.

"I wonder why he wasn't wearing a mask, like the others?"

"Because it didn't matter," Diesel said. "He wouldn't

survive anyway."

"What do you mean?"

"He was targeted to not survive," he said, "as in, once his mask came off, the others couldn't afford to let him live."

"But even by association," she said, "if you find who one is, surely you can track down the others."

"Unless they were hired out, using locals," Diesel said. He brought up his laptop and started typing away.

"What's he doing?" she asked, looking at Shane.

"Contacting our group to see if anybody has any information," he said.

When Diesel lifted his head, he shook it and said, "The two bad guys left in the building are still unconscious. And the cabbie isn't talking."

"Interesting," she said. "Maybe we should knock him out a little bit more. When they wake up, knock them out again if they won't talk."

"Hard to get answers from an unconscious guy," Shane said.

"Sure, but it's much easier on our tempers."

He snorted. "You can't just go in and wring their necks if they don't want to talk."

"Why not?" she said. "I never did understand that."

"It's about fair treatment."

"But if you put a gun in their hands, how fair would their treatment of us be?"

"Not at all fair," Shane said, as he looked at Diesel, busy pounding on the keyboard.

When he looked up, Diesel said, "I've asked for information on any SEAL groups taken out in the last year."

"Revenge is best served cold," she said. "So, if you're referring back to what I was saying, go back at least three or four years."

He looked at her, surprised, then shrugged and typed into the keyboard again.

As soon as she finished eating, she got up and walked to the bathroom.

Shane cleared off a spot for his laptop, then opened the Mavericks chat window. In the chat, he asked for access to all cameras in the city, particularly those around the telecom building. As soon as that link came up, he started going through the cameras in the building itself. But they were all shut down at the time. When Shelly rejoined them, he asked her, "Did you have any argument with anybody in the telecom building?"

"Nope," she said from the bed. I wasn't there long enough to get to know anybody, much less make enemies."

"No, but you have a tendency to piss people off," he said. "They generally love you or hate you, and it doesn't take them long to decide."

"Lately it's been more about hate," she said.

He looked to find her arms under her head, as she stared up at the ceiling. "Tell me about it," he said.

"Nothing much to tell," she said, "but apparently some-body else in the building wanted my job. Don't know his name. Management didn't bother to tell him, so, when he found out I got it, he wasn't very happy."

"Did you see him at some point in time afterward?"

"Every day," she said. "I had to go up the same elevator with him every day."

"Was he difficult to live with?"

"Yes," she said. "He used to make derogatory remarks all the time. It was obviously sour grapes, but still it gets to be irritating. I tried to avoid him, even changing the time I would show up at work, in order to avoid seeing him, and things like that."

"Do you think he could be behind any of this?"

"But then you're making this about me," she said, rolling to look at him, "when it's really all about you."

Diesel snorted at that. "She's got a good way to put things back in perspective."

"She does," Shane grumped.

"That's nothing new," she said, yawning. She curled up, her hands under her head, as she studied the two men working.

"We'll get to the bottom of it," he said. "I just need you to stay low and out of trouble while it happens."

"Says you," she said. "At least I don't have a job to show up to tomorrow."

"But do you even know that? Maybe they would just relegate you to another department."

"There is no other department," she said. "Well, at least not one with a job I'm qualified for."

"Do they have another building anywhere in the city?"

"Yes, but again not in my field."

"Maybe we should take a look at the personnel records of everybody you worked with."

"You're putting it back on me again," she said. "This isn't about me. Remember?"

"Maybe," he said. "Or maybe that was a diversionary tactic."

"No," she said, "they were talking about you. I heard them say it."

"What exactly did you hear?" he asked, and both he and Diesel turned to look at her.

She opened her sleepy eyes, stared at them, and said,

"There were talking among themselves, and I heard them say your name."

"What name?"

"They said Shane. He actually made it sound pretty disgusting. Then he said I was your girlfriend, well, your 'doxy,' he said." She snorted at that. "As if I'm anybody's doxy. Do you believe that?"

"Back to the conversation," he said, leaning forward. "Think back now, and tell me exactly what they said."

She closed her eyes and thought about it for a moment. "Two guys were off to the side, saying that I was the important one and that you would only come for your doxy," she said with emphasis. "He said, 'Shane'll only come for his doxy. They've been best friends since forever.'"

"So he already knew something about us then?" Shane said, frowning.

"Yeah, but then the other man said, 'There's no way,' and the first man said, 'Yes. You don't understand the relationship. I do.'"

At that, Shane let out a slow deep breath. "So who do we know that knows about us?" he asked, staring at her quietly. "Because, although we've been friends for a long time," he said, "we haven't shared mutual friends together for that whole time."

Her eyes widened, and she slowly sat up again. "That is very true. How many people do we know in common? And how many people have you actually told about us? I don't tell anybody," she said. "It's just between the two of us. We used to have mutual friends, but it was way back when though, like in grade school."

"Right, so how many names can you come up with of people who know about us?"

She thought about it and said, "Sam and Jimmy," she said. "We used to go out with them sometimes."

"Right, and both of them are in England right now."

She raised her eyebrows. "Are they?" She shrugged. "I didn't know that."

"Who else?"

"Well, there's Deborah," she said. "But I know she's fat and sassy with her fourth pregnancy right now."

"Fourth?" he repeated, his tone rising.

She winced and said, "Yeah, four. She just keeps popping them out."

"As long as she's happy, I guess," he said doubtfully.

She laughed. "Hey, just because neither of us have been into the whole multiple-kid thing doesn't mean other people don't want it."

"I just can't imagine," he said. "Okay, so anybody else you can think of?"

"What about people we may have come across through work?" she replied.

"Did you tell anybody about me?"

She shrugged. "I wouldn't think so. I don't know," she said. "I have known you a lot of years."

"True," he said. "Did the gunmen say anything else?"

"Only something along the lines of they needed to just be patient, and you would come."

"Which is very true. Were there any comments from them about how I would come, or what training I had? Anything?"

"No," she said. "Just that—" She looked at him and said, "One of them said, 'I've waited a long time.'"

"Ah," he said. "So there is something that goes back a long time in this scenario." He looked at Diesel and back to

Shelly. "I wonder how much somebody would have to hate me to do something like this?"

"They don't have to hate you very much," she said wondering how long until she could get her purse and phone back. "They just have to hate you enough. And usually that involves somebody else."

"Meaning?"

CHAPTER 5

"**I** CAN'T IMAGINE anybody hating you that much in a personal sense," Shelly said. "So I'm imagining it's probably something more oriented to your job. Or someone they lost because of you."

"Diesel?"

"I don't know, man. It's hard to say," Diesel said. "How about we try to get some descriptions."

"Good idea. I don't know why we didn't do this before."

"We started, then never came back to it. There's really been no time," she said, comfortably curling up again. "You'll have to ask fast, before I fall asleep, though."

"Okay. Height?"

Her eyes popped open. "Of what," she asked, looking confused.

"The four guys. Or however many you saw."

"I saw them all. Well, I saw four anyway. One was shorter, the unmasked guy, who I saw but just briefly," she said. "The other three were tall, and actually two of them looked like they could have been brothers. They both had dark hair, dark beards, darker skin, of similar height and build." She frowned. "I'll say a little bit shorter than you. So maybe just over six foot or so."

"Build?"

"Well, the two brothers were slim. Not a whole lot of

beef on them. The third one was the odd man out."

"Was he likely to be the boss or just another lackey?"

"More of the boss," she said, "but honestly all four could have been lackeys. They all could have been hired to do this."

"They probably were," he said. "The question we have to answer is why. But in order to do that, I need to see the people." Shane turned to Diesel. "Did you find anything on the cameras?"

"I'm still looking," he said, "there are a lot of city cameras."

"Yeah. Do you have anything from the sky?" she asked curiously.

He looked at her and frowned. "What do you mean?"

"Well, the only way for them to have gotten out was helicopters, right?"

"That's one of the more obvious ways, yes."

"The third man, the odd man out," she said, picturing him in her mind, "he was blond, shorter, and much more heavyset, but my sense is that he was pretty heavily muscled. He had a really big jaw on him."

"Any accent?"

"Not that I could tell," she said. "They all spoke English."

"Limps, tattoos, or disfigurations?"

She shook her head. "Nothing that I saw," she said. "We didn't get a great look though, and then we were shoved into the one room, until I was singled out."

"So you didn't know what happened to the others, your coworkers?"

"No," she said. "Nothing. Mary was the only one I saw, once they separated me. I didn't hear the shots that took out my coworkers. I didn't see or hear anything else," she said then another thought hit. "I hope she has someone to look after her cats."

"We'll make sure the police know about them." Shane said. "If you think of anything else, let us know." Then he turned back to his laptop.

"What are you looking at?" she asked.

"I'm looking for neighboring buildings that are higher up that I might access cameras from."

"Honestly there didn't seem to be anything remarkable or memorable about them, other than the murders. They came upon us so quickly. The front door opened, and the receptionist came into the back area where we were all working. The gunman was holding a gun against her head, and they pushed us all into the one room. Then, like I said, I was singled out and taken off into another room. Other than that, I didn't see anything," she said, "until Mary was brought in."

"Why Mary?"

"She was the older motherly type," she said, "and we had been a little friendlier than the others."

"Do you think they knew that?"

"A couple questions would have shown that to them," she said. "So I have no idea if she volunteered that info or if somebody else said something to the gunmen."

"Okay, so that's a dead end," Shane said, frowning. "I'm still struggling to find cameras, and they stopped—whoa, hang on." He adjusted his laptop, as Diesel headed to look over his shoulder.

"What's up?"

"What did you find?" she asked.

"The helicopter that took them off the building," he

said. Immediately he typed in the call numbers on the bird. "We'll find out who owns that chopper right now," he said. "It's hard to see, but it looks like two men getting on."

"The big question is still the same," Diesel said. "What the hell is this all about?"

"I wonder what they planned to do when you got there?" she asked. "Would they take you away or would they just shoot you?"

He nodded. "Thankfully they didn't get that chance."

"Maybe it was a test. Both men looked at her, wearing puzzled expressions. She shrugged. "I don't know," she said, "but, for all we know, they wanted you for something else. Maybe it wasn't about revenge. Maybe it was more to see if you could do the job."

"*Huh.*" Diesel turned and looked at Shane and said, "I actually like that idea. Just think about it. If you got her out of there safely, that could stand as proof of your competence."

"But they killed how many people to make that test happen?" Shane asked, frowning. "And what about his words, 'I've waited a long time for this'?"

"They had to make it believable," Diesel said. Just then Gavin replied in the chat window.

Helicopter is owned by a rental company. It was rented out for four days by a mining company that denies ordering the rental, although they confirmed that a company credit card was used. They have reported it as a fraudulent transaction.

"Great, so they assume the identity of another company and use it for the rental. Nobody knows who's used it, and they've had access to wheels or wings for that time period," he said. "Probably to hire local gunmen. Smart."

"It confuses the issue, for sure."

"Which seems to be a theme in this whole deal," she said. "It's like they're keeping everything confused and off balance, so nobody knows up from down."

"And doing a pretty good job of it," Shane said in frustration.

"Maybe that's part of the test too," she said.

"If it is, I'm damn tired of being tested," he snapped.

As he glared at her, she held up her hands, palms out. "I get it," she said. "Maybe, just maybe, they want something to do with you."

"Maybe," he said. "I just don't understand what."

"And, if that were the case," Diesel said, "they would contact you."

"Maybe," she said. "The question is, in what way?"

"I didn't even get contacted over the kidnapping," Shane said suddenly. "The Mavericks did." He quickly sent a message to Gavin. **Any other communication regarding this scenario? Specifically, have the kidnappers contacted you?**

Not yet, Gavin said. **What are you thinking?** Shane quickly filled in Gavin on the other possibility they had been kicking around.

It's possible, but I don't like the idea in the least. To even think that we were being tested for something like this is a bit much.

But we've seen things like that before.

Well, we all have job interviews but hardly in this way.

Gavin, do you know of any sensitive cases worldwide that might need somebody for a job like that?

Now that you mention it, yes. There was silence on the chat for a moment and then a link was posted. **The**

73

missing daughter of one of the international oil tycoons.

He's got his own team though. He'd get his daughter out on his own, Shane wrote, as Shelly and Diesel looked on over his shoulder.

"Not to mention that she's a female," Shelly said. Frowning, the guys looked at her, and she shrugged. "I know that, in some cultures, women have value, but, in others, they don't. I'm not sure on this one."

Wait.

Shane sat back. "Gavin's got something." Moments later another message popped up in the chat.

Check out the email I just forwarded to you.

It was a message addressed to the head of the Mavericks Department, which he didn't even know existed. It was written in code, and it was a message to Gavin, saying Shane was needed for a specialized job.

"Hang on a minute. What the hell are they talking about?" he asked, trying to understand the missive. His phone rang just then, a call from Gavin. Shane put it on Speaker.

"Shane, this is a telecommunication missive encode that just came through our system," he said. "And you're right. They do want you for a job. But take a deep breath. You won't like the price."

"What's the price?" he asked, his stomach churning.

"They are holding your sister and her family."

"What are you talking about?" he cried out, bolting to his feet.

"It says, they will hold your family, until you get the tycoon's daughter back."

"So what's all this about Shelly then?"

"A test run."

"What the hell? A test run where they killed eleven people," he said in the harsh voice. "Why me?"

"The story for the Mavericks is that he was somehow associated with one of your black ops years ago," Gavin said. "He had a contact, supposedly in a unit that handled the communications for one of your SEAL teams," he said. "So, when his family ran into trouble, he decided he needed you guys. That last part may be true, but the guy is probably the international oil tycoon. Everybody else has refused to help him, and he's tried several others but with no luck. He wondered if you had the skills."

"How long has the daughter been missing?"

"Five months."

"Jesus. How many has he tested?"

"Unfortunately he's not responding to that question," he said, "but I'm looking it up."

"I don't have a good feeling about this. So he's up against somebody, and he's looking for people capable of getting her back. So he's already tested and tried several, and what? I'm the next one on the list?"

"Possibly," Gavin said. "You were also out of the loop for a long time and may have been harder to get a hold of."

"Maybe so but this is all bullshit."

"Not to mention the fact that a lot of people have already died from whatever game he's playing," she said.

"I hear you there," Shane said. He looked at Diesel, who just stared at him in shock.

"Are you serious?" Diesel asked. "They killed eleven innocent people in a communications office trying to get some help?"

"Looks like it," Gavin said.

"Well, that's complete bullshit, and I'm not doing it," Shane said.

"Well, you may want to take a look at this." Gavin sent through a link on the chat.

Shane turned back to his laptop and clicked the link. Sure enough, there was his sister, her two kids, and her husband, all sitting at the dining room table, with frozen smiles on their faces, a gunman on either side of the room. "Jesus Christ," he said, pinching the bridge of his nose.

"Sorry, Shane," Gavin said.

"You know what? You don't really think about jobs that you work on. We don't even know when we crossed paths with an oil sheikh or if he was a second-tier casualty in some way," he said. "For all I know, he learned of me from a job years ago."

"It may well have been," Gavin said. "I'm still trying to get information."

"And obviously this isn't somebody we'd want to work for, if he has to use this kind of leverage."

"I'm assuming that's exactly why he's using this kind of leverage. It's the only thing he can do to get help."

"Which means, he has friends in high places, plus money and other connections, to get what he needs from people like him. Just not from people like us."

"That's my take too," Diesel said. "Hell, I don't want to deal with him either."

"No," Shane said, "not the way he's operated." He said to Gavin, "I won't deal while he's got my family," he said. "I was tested and apparently passed, but no way I'll be held accountable for what'll happen when I get a hold of him if he hurts my sister."

"I hear you," Gavin said, "and you know we don't cooperate with blackmailers," he said, "which means that now it becomes an operation to rescue your sister."

"That is the only thing I'm prepared to do," he said. "Then I'll take this asshole out in an alleyway and make sure he never pulls a stunt like this with my family again."

She couldn't believe what she heard, as she stared at the link on the laptop and shuddered. "They look so scared."

IT HURT TO look at his sister and see the terror in her eyes. Shane had to save them. He couldn't live with anything else. "Gavin, have you got anybody close to San Diego, who can go over there to check out my sister's house?"

"Yeah, they've been on the move, while we've been talking," he said. "They've set up a perimeter on the house. Can you confirm the location, just to be safe?" He then read off the address.

"Yeah, that's her place."

"Well, give us a minute to do a quick search," he said. "The house is dark, so we can't be sure if they're inside or not."

"If the kidnappers are smart, they took them far away," he said, his voice raw. "But, if not," he said, "we'll make sure we get them out of there."

Just then another call rang on his phone. As soon as he disconnected with Gavin, the new call rang and rang. He stared down at the number, wrote it down, and then answered. Instinct had him saying, "What the fuck do you want?"

"You," said the harsh voice on the other side.

"After you killed all those people, hurt my friend, and

took my family captive?"

A short pause came from the other end. "You are fast," he said. "Good, that's what I need."

"That may be what you need," he said, "but your methodology leaves a lot to be desired."

"Maybe," he said, "but, if I'd asked you, would you have helped?"

"No," he said.

"I've asked lots of people in the last few months," he said, "and nobody's willing to help."

"So what's the pressure now?"

"They've given me ten days, or they'll kill her."

"You just killed eleven people for nothing," he said. "Why would I want to help you, after you took all those innocent lives?"

"I had to know if you could do the job," he said. "Everybody else has failed."

"Well, that's bullshit," he said. "I'm really not into death missions either."

"And that's possible," he said, "but I'm desperate."

"And your daughter? Do you know that she's even still alive?"

"She is but not for long," he said, his voice raw. "She's the only child I have," he said. "She told me four years ago to get out of the business, and I didn't do it, and now somebody went after her. That's inexcusable."

"Oh, trust me. I know how you feel," he snapped. "Because you've just gone after my family," he said, "and there will be a reckoning at the end of this."

"I don't give a damn," he said. "Shoot me if you can, but I want to make sure my daughter lives."

"Yet you're hurting so many others without a care."

"If it was your daughter, wouldn't you?" And, with that, he hung up.

Shane quickly put the number into the chat for Gavin and quickly wrote about the call.

Jesus Christ, Gavin said. **The house is empty.**

Shane buried his face in his hands for a moment, as he thought about what this meant. Immediately he felt soft hands rest on his shoulders. He reached up a hand and covered Shelly's with his.

"I'm sorry you got pulled into all this," she said.

He shook his head. "Hey, this is just part and parcel of the industry I work in," he said. "I'm just sorry for all the people who have been dragged into it."

"But it's not your fault," she said.

"Try telling that to my sister."

"You'll get them back," she said.

He snorted. "I don't even know where the guy's daughter is being held."

Almost immediately he received a text message on his phone from the same number. It contained an address and a simple message. **My daughter's in the basement.**

He stared at it and said, "Jesus Christ, she's in London."

At that, Diesel hopped to his feet and came around to have a look. He wrote down the address and said, "Okay, let me get onto that." He sat back down and soon accessed old blueprints and schematics on the building. "It was an old government building that was sold privately at some point," he said, "but, as such, it's got security all through it."

"Do we know who owns it?" Shane asked.

"Looks like an Iranian corporation," Diesel said, "Imports and exports."

Shane rolled his eyes at that. "Great."

"What's wrong with imports and exports?" Shelly asked.

"Let's just say, it can cover a multitude of sins," Diesel said.

She nodded. "So, what can I do?"

"Well, now that we know it's not about you—"

"Oh, come on," she said. "If there's something I can do to help you, let me help."

"There's really nothing you can do," Shane said. "But, at the same time, I can't let you go back home again either. That won't be safe."

"Why not?" she asked, and he looked up to see genuine curiosity.

"In case I screw up, or if I want to back out, they have my family, but I've already proven that I would come after you," he said. "So they'll pick you up, if they get another chance too."

She sat down, thinking about it. "So, what size operation does a guy like this have?"

"Huge," he said and stared at her. "Why?"

"Is it really possible then that nobody knows about him?"

"Absolutely," he said. "Anybody like him, who deals in black market arms or in any kind of illegal front, will have all kinds of privacy that he's bought and paid for."

"Right," she said. "I feel useless without my laptop." Walking to her bag, she pulled it out and hooked it up. "I'll do some research on my own."

"Fine," he said, "just share what you find."

"Will do." She hooked it up, sat down, and started thinking about the little bits and pieces she had learned. Then she looked into kidnappings reported in the media from six months ago. "Why six months ago, and why now?

There's got to be a reason for now."

"They want something from him," Shane said, and Diesel nodded in agreement. "That's the only reason for the time frame to move up. He's been arguing with the kidnapper. As long as they kept his daughter safe, he was going along with it. Now they've asked for something bigger, and he won't budge. So he's got to get her out of there, before he's pushed to the limit."

"Yes, that makes a lot of sense." Mulling that over, she continued her search. A few minutes later she found something. "That company was sold several months ago," she said.

"Sold by who? And who bought it?" Shane asked.

"From the Iranian import-export company, like Diesel said, to a British one. It was sold six months ago. The original company still owns the building."

"Which would be around the time that she was picked up," he said. "The kidnappers may have bought it just to hold her there."

"Or the new buyer is just a shell corporation for the Iranian import-export company," Shane suggested.

"Regardless of who owns it now, can you guys get any schematics on it?" Shelly asked.

"Yeah, I already have them up," Diesel said. "It's a pretty straightforward three-story building, with underground docks."

"Underground?" she asked.

"One level belowground for trucking," he said.

"More than one way in or out?" Shane asked.

"Several," he said, tapping the screen. "Heavy security installed."

"What's around it?" Shane asked.

"Looks like industrial sites," Diesel replied. "What's on your mind?"

"Is there anything butted up against it, with a shared wall, that we could maybe drill through or something like that?"

Diesel smiled and looked at him with respect. "Yeah, give me a second to take a look here." He scrolled around, carefully looking at the adjacent buildings. "Okay, looks like a manufacturing plant is beside it on the left. An alley on the back and some kind of metal fabrication shop on the other side."

"But isn't that too easy?" Shelly asked.

"The place will be wired in some way, no doubt," Diesel said with a nod. "It would be good to get Gavin to check for security on the street and adjacent buildings."

"On it," Shane said, and bringing up the chat, he quickly asked for any available security feeds on the street and around the corner. **We'll need it for the last six months, but I want it in one-month segments, and I need the last twenty-four hours ASAP. I'll also need passage to England, as fast as possible.** Then he started typing again. **Flights preferred. London.**

It wasn't long before Gavin replied. **We can have you out in the morning.**

Put us on the first flight out then, Shane replied. He looked to see Shelly curled up and already asleep now. **Better make it for three.**

A question mark came back from Gavin, so Shane grabbed the phone and gave him a call. "I don't dare leave her behind. I don't want to give these assholes any more leverage than what we already know they have on me."

"Got it. I understand."

Shane stopped and thought for a moment. "Hey, Gavin, who the hell is paying for this anyway?"

"Does it matter?"

"Well, it's my family being held, and I'm the one being extorted to do something, though I seem to be dragging the rest of you along with me."

"Look, Shane, let's just get through it. We can do any settling up later, if we need to, after we have all the facts. We're trying to get more information on what's going on and on what group we're dealing with. MI6 has been contacted. They're not impressed that you're coming, by the way."

"Of course not," he said. "I had a few dealings with one of the MI6 agents a few years ago."

"Yeah, he's had some dealings with a lot of us," Gavin said, and a round of laughter could be heard on the other end.

Shane just smiled and said, "They'll deal. They don't want these guys in their lives either." When he finally hung up, Diesel sat there, watching Shane.

"You okay, man?"

"Yeah, I'm okay," Shane said. "Pissed off and worried about my family."

"I don't think they'll be in London."

"No," he said, "he'll have them squirreled away somewhere else. That'll be a whole other operation to deal with." He exhaled. "After seeing what this guy did with his testing process, I'm sure he'd kill them in a heartbeat if I fail to get his daughter out, and we need to make sure that that doesn't happen."

"I've got the photos that he originally sent us. I presume it's her house?" Diesel asked.

Shane got up and walked around, so he could look at the

images over Diesel's shoulder. "Yes," he said. "That's her house."

"So, where are they being held is the next question."

"And there is just no way to know," he said, sitting back down with a *thump*. "So we need to prioritize here. We'll start with what we'll do about my sister and also look at the London location where the daughter is and make a plan. Especially how we'll deal with the explosives."

At that, Diesel's head came up. "Explosives?"

Shane gave him a crooked smile. "It's one of the reasons I was picked, I'm guessing," he said. "I'm an explosives expert."

"You must have gotten into that after our last SEALs mission together, huh?"

"Oh, yeah, maybe so," he said. "Yeah, I got a lot of detailed training, then did a lot of work in that field. Actually that may be why our paths haven't crossed for a while. It was one of the things I was happy to let go of when I walked away."

"I'm not so sure we ever really walk away," Diesel said.

"Obviously," Shane said, with a motion toward their laptops. "So we need to know everything about the vehicle that came and took my sister's family away. And we need access to the camera feeds for that."

"I requested the feeds earlier, so I've had a chance to check them out. I found one likely vehicle, a black delivery-style van. The license plates return to a stolen vehicle taken about four months ago," he said.

"Wow," Shane said. "They're playing a long game here."

"Well, either it was stolen on the off chance they would need it or it's been something they've been using here and there, and, so far, they haven't been caught with it."

"Maybe," he said, "but I really don't trust this asshole,

and I have no sympathy for him. He just happens to have an even bigger asshole cranking his chain. We have to make sure that, by the end of the day, we're the ones holding all the damn chains."

"I got it," Diesel said, "and I'm really sorry about your family."

"I appreciate that," he said, "but I have to set aside the grieving and focus on the mission. We'll share some barbecue when this is over, when we have my sister and her family with us."

"You got it, man," he said, "and you still owe me one steak already, by the way."

Shane snorted with laughter at that. "Find out where she is, and figure out how we'll save them," he said, "and I'll upgrade you and get you the biggest damn steak you've ever seen." With that, they each settled in and got to work.

They both worked silently for a time; then Diesel sat back and stretched. "I caught sight of that van heading toward the airport," Diesel said, "but it veers off beforehand."

"Well, the camera spot-checks all along the line," Shane said. "So keep tracking, and you should run it down."

"Yeah, I was hoping to get lucky and track it quickly, but no such luck."

"We can't make an attack too fast," Shane said. "But I would love to have them safe before this goes down."

"Preferably so you can tell this other guy to take a hike," Diesel said.

He nodded; then he thought about it and winced. "I know, right? Yet I keep thinking about this woman, who's been held captive for six months. How could I walk away knowing what she's going through?"

CHAPTER 6

S HELLY HAD HEARD part of the conversation but was still struggling to process some of it. "I'll fly to London with you?"

"Yeah. Otherwise you're staying here in a safe house," he said, his tone brooking no argument.

She just shook her head in bewilderment. "But I'm safe now," she said. "You'll go off and rescue this woman and save your sister, which, ... oh, my God, how the hell is Priscilla handling this now?" she asked, worried. "I'm so worried about the kids."

"She's a lawyer. I'm sure she's calm and controlled at the moment. But, like anybody, it's her children and her husband at risk with her," Shane said. "Nice diversion by the way. Now back to the matter at hand. We can't take any chances of them grabbing you again."

"A safe house?"

"A safe house *under guard*," he said affirmatively.

"And if I go to London with you?"

"Then you'll be with me at all times, except for when I'm off doing an op."

She stared at him, warring with the two options, but there was really no choice. "All right, I'm coming with you then," she said.

He nodded. "I figured that would be your choice. We

leave for the airport in forty minutes. Get up and get showered. Breakfast will be delivered any minute."

She slowly pushed back the blankets and sat up, still brushing the grogginess of sleep from her eyes, as she headed for the shower. "London? Wow." Well, there were worse things. She thought about the woman he was supposed to rescue, and her heart went out to the poor soul. Yet, at the same time, eleven people had been killed as a trial run, and she had absolutely no doubt that this guy was planning on taking care of Shane and Diesel and her at the end of the day.

But, if he would do that and kill her regardless, Shelly didn't think a safe house would be safer than being with these two. She trusted them, and, right now, she didn't trust many people, particularly not after the experience of getting into that cab. Showered, dressed, and back out in the main room, she quickly packed up her overnight bag and stared at it sorrowfully. "I guess there's no time for a side trip to pick up more clothes, is there?"

"In your dreams," he said cheerfully. "Wander around in your underwear. I don't care."

She snorted at that. "Yeah, you wouldn't have a problem with that at all, would you?" she said, shaking her head. "Not happening."

"Bedsheets work," Diesel said unhelpfully, with a wicked grin.

She rolled her eyes at him. "Maybe in London I can shop." They just looked at her, then looked at each other and didn't say anything, which she took to mean, *No way in hell was that happening*. She groaned and said, "You could have warned me."

"We didn't know beforehand," he said, and a tap on the

door stopped the conversation. He immediately motioned for her to step back. Eyes wide, she hid behind the corner, as Diesel walked to the front door.

"Who's there?" he called out.

"Room service."

He opened the door slightly, checking out who was there to ensure it truly was room service, then opened the door wider. "I'll take the trolley from here." Diesel tipped the guy, shut the door, and pushed the trolley farther inside.

She lifted her nose, appreciating the smell of bacon. "Bacon is always a good choice," she murmured.

"It is," Shane said. "Come and eat." He lifted up the bottom tray, which held a big coffee server, and set it on the table.

Once served, they sat down, and she quickly demolished her food. "Okay, that was a good start," she said. "I have to admit that you shocked me with the change in plans."

"You need to be adaptable," he said. "You chose to come with us, then you need to be prepared to do as we tell you, without arguments and questions. We can answer your questions eventually, but, in the moment, you just need to do as you're told."

She looked at him, smiled, and said, "I'll only do it because I know that you love me."

Putting down his fork, he gripped her fingers. "You know that," he said. "So when you don't like what I tell you, remember what's behind it."

She grinned and snagged the last piece of toast off the plate. "I'll remember." He looked down at the plate, then back at her in mock outrage. She shrugged and took a big bite of it. "Hey, you took more bacon than me," she said.

"I'm bigger than you," he said reasonably.

"Sure," she said, "but you don't want to be sitting on that long flight with me cranky and hungry."

"Oh, God, you're right about that," he said. "You're the worst." He pushed his chair back and said, "I need to check in for more information," he said. "Then we're leaving in five." He walked over, snagged his phone, and stepped out on a small balcony. There he proceeded to tap his phone, with text messages presumably.

She looked at Diesel. "Are you two working out? Like, as partners, I mean. Are you okay to work with him?"

The corner of his lips kicked up into a grin. "Always," he said. "I trust him."

"Oh, I do too," she said. "I just can't say that I've ever been in a scenario like this."

"Not a problem," he said. "But, seriously, you've got to listen to what we say and just do it without argument."

"Why does everybody keep saying that?" She wrinkled her nose at him. "I get that I probably seem a little more argumentative than other people," she said cautiously, "but I do know when to be quiet."

"I was in that cab," he said. "I saw your attempt to be quiet."

She burst out laughing at that. "Hey, the guy was trying to kidnap us. After the hostage situation, what did you expect me to do?"

"Well, we were in the process of handling it," he said, "but then you got in the way, and we couldn't do what we were trying to do."

She stopped, stared at him, and said, "Oh. I didn't even think about that."

"Which is exactly why you need to do what we tell you to do."

She shrugged and said, "Well, I'll try."

He rolled his eyes at her.

"Yeah, yeah, yeah," she said. "If you've been around Shane for any amount of time, you would know perfectly well what I'm like," she said.

"He doesn't talk about you," he said quietly.

She looked at him and smiled "No, I guess not. We've always kept this relationship pretty private. I can't remember anybody else I might have told," she said. "That's the problem with trying to figure out who might have spread the word about how tight we are. Good thing we know about the origin of this mess now. Although finding out about me is a little confusing."

"It doesn't necessarily have to be anybody you guys told. It could be where you have been seen together or something like that. Particularly since your friendship is long and enduring. Think about anything that could still be on the internet."

She stared at him thoughtfully. "In that case," she said, "there are probably dozens and dozens of photos of us. We went to various celebrations, concerts, expos." She shrugged. "We're friends."

"Exactly. And you've shown up together, time and time again, right?"

She nodded. "Yeah, even when he had girlfriends, I'd be there," she said. "Or, if I had boyfriends, sometimes he'd be there too. We're friends."

"Exactly. So think about that. If someone was trying to find somebody in his life worth kidnapping …"

"But only as a test," she said, shaking her fork at him. "His sister was the leverage."

"Well, it's both. That was his test, and now they've got

leverage."

"It would be a good idea, you know, if you guys would grab this woman and keep her as leverage, so Shane can get his sister's family back."

"Well, that's plan B," he said, standing up. "Plan A is to get his family back first," he said. "Believe me. This guy won't get his daughter back without us getting Shane's family back first."

"I'm glad to hear you say that," she said. "I really like Prissy."

"You're probably the only one I know who's even met them."

"And again," she said, "as much as by accident, just because we've been friends for a long time."

"Has it really been since kindergarten?"

"Yes, actually it has. Some years we were closer than other times, but yes."

"Hard to imagine that you knew him before he went in the navy."

"Yes, when I was like sixteen, we spent a lot of time together," she said. "Prissy is a couple years older. She's a bit more straitlaced than he is. But then he was a wild card."

"Got it," he said with a smile.

"Come on. Let's go," Shane said, stepping back inside the room.

She looked up in surprise. Shane already stood at the doorway, waiting for them. She hopped up, took one last gulp of her coffee, and swallowed it. "Wow," she said, "I was hoping for another cup."

"Maybe at the airport," Shane said.

She nodded, grabbed her bag and her sweater, and said, "Okay, I'm ready."

He smiled and said, "Let's hope so," and led the way outside.

She was surprised when they didn't go down the stairwell or the normal elevator. They went down another elevator, set off all by itself, which was darker inside. "Where are we?" she murmured.

"Service elevator," he said. As soon as they stepped out in an underground parking area at a dark corner, he grabbed her arm and tugged her back.

"You could always walk behind me." She sighed, and, pulling her arm away, said, "You do know that this is the modern-day, and women no longer have to walk behind their partner."

He said, "From this second forward, you will definitely be without the right to vote, argue, or disobey. Otherwise I'm not taking you. You'll be under guard at a safe house. So you better decide right here and now." His voice was hard.

She gently patted his back and said, "I'm right here—behind you."

He reached back, and she grabbed his hand and let him lead her toward a black car with smoked windows. He quickly settled her into the back, as Diesel got in the driver's seat. Shane sat in the front passenger side, so she had the whole back seat to herself.

She didn't really recognize this persona of his but certainly understood where he was coming from. She settled back for the trip to the airport. They didn't even enter through the normal doors but ended up using some godforsaken back entrance. She passed all kinds of carts and a few people, but most of them didn't look like they were travelers. But suddenly they were through inspections and walking toward the plane. "How did you bypass everybody like that?"

"We didn't bypass anything," he said, "but whenever you have law enforcement heading out or carrying passengers," he said, "you always move through a different set of security measures."

"Am I a prisoner now?"

"No, but the weapons we're carrying," he said, "are definitely part of it."

"You got permission to carry these?"

"Most are in the checked luggage," he said, "but we have permission for one each on board."

"Jesus," she said, "does that make you an air marshal or something?"

"No, but you can bet they know that Diesel and I are here," he said. "Only nobody is allowed to say a word."

"Interesting," she murmured. As it was, they found their seats, and they were in the center section instead of at the front or at the back, and she was in the middle, between the two of them. She figured that's just the way it would be from now on. "Is it okay if I sleep on this flight?"

"Yeah, sleep all you want," he said, "Diesel and I will be working."

"What's to work on?" she asked in surprise.

He looked at her, his lips kicking up in the corners, and he said, "We have plans to make."

"Well, with that heavy breakfast this morning, I'm already yawning again."

"That's just because you didn't get your extra cup of coffee," he teased.

"It is," she said. "I can always get one when we're airborne, I guess."

"You could," he said, "or you can wait for a few hours and have a nap first."

"Maybe, I'll see," she said. As it was, by the time they were in the air, she felt completely exhausted. It must have been the shock and the adrenaline loss finally catching up to her. The seat belt sign hadn't been off for five minutes, and she had curled up against Shane's shoulder, her eyes closed, and drifted off.

SHANE WAS HAPPY when Shelly finally crashed.

Diesel looked at her and said, "I still think I'm right."

"You're not," Shane said. "I don't want to risk losing the friendship."

"Taking a friendship another step forward," Diesel said gently, "should enhance the friendship."

"I know, and I would be lying if I didn't say that I hadn't considered it over the years," he said, "but it always comes back to the same thing. I don't want to lose her."

"I get it, but I think you're worried about that for nothing."

"Maybe so," he said, "but I know, for a fact, that what we have now is worth everything."

"You already love her," Diesel said.

"Maybe," he said. "No, of course I do. But as a friend."

Diesel just snorted quietly. "You keep on telling yourself that, bro."

"Any luck with a potential route to get into that building?"

"No," Diesel said. "I'm now checking several buildings away at this point."

"And I'm still looking for anything related to where they could be holding my sister."

"At this point, Shelly may well prove correct."

Shane glanced at the sleeping woman between them. "What point was that?"

"She said that you'll have to rescue this woman first, then hold her captive, until your family is released."

He nodded and shrugged. "You know something? Shelly's very good at quickly grasping the salient facts," he said. "And she's right. The way it's looking, unless we catch a break pretty soon, that's probably what we'll have to do. I was hoping for more information on finding my family because no way in hell I would be heading for London if it wouldn't get me what I wanted eventually, which is my family back."

"That's what I figured. Still, that was a pretty rough trial to test your skills."

"The whole thing is strange. He said I passed with flying colors. So he's hoping that I'll get this woman out of there."

"I know. We must find a way to get in and to get her out of there, then avoid an ambush that would take her away from us."

"I'd go underground," Shane said, "if I thought a viable route was found there."

"Well, I'm into the underground city of London," he said. "It's a bit messy, well, a lot messy," he said, "but it might be our only way."

"I think it probably is," Shane said. "We may need a delivery truck going to one of the neighboring districts to get in, so nobody can track us. Then find a way to get as close to these buildings as we can. But I think we'll have to drill a pathway upward to get where we want to go."

"Not if I can find something old in that system that will get us closer," Diesel said. "Drilling'll be noisy. C-4 will be noisy. Everything'll leave a mess, and we need to ensure that we don't leave very much in the way of tracks."

"We don't want to leave any tracks on our way in," Shane said, "but I don't give a shit about tracks on the way out. Once we get clear of the underground city, then we need another series of ways to get the hell out of the city itself."

"You got any plans for that?"

"Yeah," he said, "I'm thinking by sea."

"How will that help us?" Diesel asked, looking at him.

"Well, for one, nobody'll take on the US Navy for four people," he said, "and, if we do it right, they won't even know we're on one of the destroyers."

"Still won't save your family."

"Well, that doesn't mean I can't leave," he said, "while I go off and do an exchange for my family."

"I think you might be right about a destroyer, if we can make that happen," he said, "but I disagree about the exchange."

"I don't know any other way to make the switch," he said.

"Your family will need to be freed back at their home or at some neutral territory, while you have proof of life on the US destroyer," he said.

"And that means this guy has got to trust me to release this woman."

"True enough," he said. "And the handoffs are always dangerous."

"We can make it happen," he said. "First, we have to get to London, and we need a game plan, preferably by the time we land."

On that note, the two returned to work. They were interrupted a couple times with deliveries of coffee and some food, but, by the time they landed in London, they had something of a plan together. It was still rough, and they would need a lot of equipment and some backup. But, as they headed through security and continued outside for a rental and then to their hotel, Shane felt a little bit better.

On the other hand, the closer and closer they got to London and to their hotel, the quieter Shelly became. "Are you all right?" he asked, looking at her as they got out.

She yawned, nodded, and said, "Yes, but the time change for transatlantic flights like this is deadly."

"It is, but you get to sit down and relax," he said.

"I can sit, but that doesn't mean I'll relax," she said.

"You might surprise yourself," he said.

CHAPTER 7

WALKING INTO THE hotel room, Shelly stopped and eyed the suite. She looked at Shane and said, "You guys must be doing well."

"There's lots of money," he said. "It's just a matter of utilizing it for what we need it for."

She didn't say anything to that, but it made sense to her. She remembered one of the lessons she had learned at a previous company, when she had asked what she had for spending money. They told her that, if she needed it, it was okay. And she realized that meant that, if she didn't need it, it wasn't okay. It was an honor system. Order what you need, and don't abuse it. She'd taken that to heart and hadn't questioned what she had needed after that. But here, she had no clue what was needed. More clothes would be nice, but she had several outfits, and she could always do laundry. She sat down in one of the big overstuffed chairs and looked around. "It's a nice suite," she said.

"We could be here for a few days," he said.

"Can you make things happen here that fast?"

He snorted. "I can make things happen here that fast," he said, "without a doubt."

She nodded slowly and said, "This is a side of you that I've never seen before."

"And you may never see it again either," he said cheerfully.

She smiled. "Actually I kind of like it."

He rolled his eyes at that. "What's to like?" he said. "It's still just me."

"Yes, but this is the work persona," she said. "I always knew the fun off-work persona before."

"Still the same guy."

She shrugged. "It is, but it isn't."

He just laughed. "Now you're making things more complicated than they need to be."

"Sorry, but it's still a fascinating look into who you are."

At that, he stopped and turned and said, "No, really. Don't misunderstand here. This is still just me."

She nodded. "I know, and I get that. It's just another side I haven't seen before." She saw that she'd worried him with this, but he didn't have time to deal with it. She waved her hand and said, "Get back to work."

He stared at her and said, "You're still bossy. You know that, right?"

"But you love me anyway," she said. "Do we get room service here?"

"Order whatever you want," he said.

She rubbed her hands together. "Oh, for a steak."

"Still on delivery? Thought you didn't like that."

She stopped and frowned. "No, you're right. It's not the same. But it would be better than a take-out order."

"It would be," he said, "but maybe leave that idea about a steak until we're done with all this."

"Then I'll walk outside and find a fish and chip shop."

"I wouldn't push it," he said. "Nobody's going out right now."

"Right," she said and groaned. "Fine, so we're back to

room service." She picked up the brochure and said, "Well, at least they have some decent choices but, wow, the prices."

"Forget about that," he said. "Just order what you want. For all of us. We'll eat it."

At that, she smiled. "Right, got it." She went through the menu, quickly ordered coffee, and then ordered a nice seafood pasta dish for everybody, with garlic bread. By the time she ordered, she said, "That'll take a little time to get here. I'll have a shower and cool down a bit."

"Go for it."

She took one last look at the two men, both sitting at the table, laptops open, moving through their phones and their laptops, totally focused on the tasks at hand. She shook her head. "This is just business as usual, I guess," she muttered.

"Nothing usual about this at all," Shane said, looking up. "But, yes, it's business, and we will handle it just like we need to."

"Right." Feeling out of sorts and not knowing why, yet still like the odd man out and unable to help, she stepped into a hot shower. After a long day of those damn transatlantic flights, it was a relief to be on dry land again. She'd slept a lot, which should help with the time change, but she knew it would take a few days for her to really adjust.

She didn't know about Shane and Diesel, but they looked like they were raring to go already. She wondered about the adrenaline required to keep going on a steady basis for a job like this. She knew what it was like, when she was on a big job, and they were setting up communication systems and marketing plans for a new company. A certain amount of adrenaline kept her going, going, going. And then, all of a sudden, it was over, and it was almost a letdown. Not a letdown in the sense that she was disappointed, but all that adrenaline had no place to go, and it took her days to recover. She figured that this was what was happening here.

She wondered what Shane planned to do when this was all over with and when the recovery happened. She'd love to spend some time with him and have a vacation or something. Hell, maybe they could go away someplace, though, when she thought about it, she hadn't been to London in years. Maybe they could just stay here for a while.

And she had to figure out what she would do about her job. When her phone buzzed, she noted an email from the cops, looking at her to answer some questions about the shootings at her old company, she winced. She hadn't told them that she had left the country. When she was dried off and dressed and returned to the main room, braiding her shoulder-length hair on the side of her head, she brought it up. "I got an email from the cops," she said. "They want me to come in for questioning."

"Well, that won't happen," Shane said.

"Didn't we get told not to leave town?" she asked.

"Nope, we did not," he murmured, but he didn't lift his head from his computer work.

"Will I be in trouble for leaving?"

"No," he said. "Forward me the email, and I'll take care of it."

Not knowing what else to do, she quickly forwarded it to him. As she'd asked for the coffee right away and for room service to deliver the meals in a little while, she was hoping the coffee was already here. She opened the front door and stepped out into the hallway, and almost instantly Shane was right there beside her. She looked up in surprise.

"I was just looking for the coffee," she said. He turned

her around gently and led her back inside. She sighed. "That bad, huh?"

"He killed eleven people as a test," he said. "How bad does it need to get?"

She winced at the reminder. "I guess I'm just out of sorts," she said. "I want to help, but there doesn't seem to be anything I can do. I don't even know how your system works, so I don't—I can't do anything," she said. "All I see is the people I used to work with, and now even looking for a new job seems wrong. It's like a betrayal of everything they went through."

"All you can do at this point in time is look after yourself," he said. "That's the one thing that's important to me. I brought you here to keep you safe. You've been through a rough time already."

She sagged into the chair. "I get that," she said, looking down at her hands and then back up at him. "I'm just not used to being idle."

"Let's put you to work then," he said, walking to the table and snatching a pad of paper and a pen. "Write down every connection between us that you could possibly think of where someone would have seen us together."

"Wow," she said. "You mean people and places?"

"Yes."

"Since kindergarten?"

"Yes."

"I can try," she said, "but that's a bit far-fetched, isn't it?"

"Maybe, maybe not," he said. "Then find all the pictures on the internet with you and I together."

As much as they had a lot in motion, they didn't have enough quite yet. Shane looked at Diesel a couple hours later. "We should have had some deliveries by now."

He looked at his watch. "I think they're on the way."

"Dammit, I don't have time for delays," Shane said. "I'll go get ready, so we can leave as soon as everything arrives."

Diesel looked at Shelly, who was nodding asleep on the bed. "What about her?"

"I've got that taken care of," he said. He looked at Diesel and winced. "I did something I wouldn't normally do," he murmured, "but we had to contact MI6 anyway."

"Ow, ouch," he said. "Stepping on their toes is getting to be a habit."

"And they are a resource we can't afford to burn," he said. "So I brought them in on it, and they're supplying an officer to look after her."

"That's actually a good solution," he said.

At that, Shane headed to the bathroom and quickly got changed. Then he swiped on a layer of some of the military's latest face paint on his exposed skin, to reduce his facial signature, until he was out of the public eye and could don his black ski mask. The trick was to be invisible, to cut down his heat signature, to stop his face from reflecting moonlight, streetlights, etc.

When he came back out, it was Diesel's turn.

Shane saw the gear that he'd ordered had arrived, as well as the officer from MI6. Shane quickly put on his bulletproof vest. Now, dressed in black from top to bottom, it would get him where he needed to go. The black gear worked best at night in cityscapes, if he kept to the shadows. Or for tunnels under the city. However, in a jungle, camo was better. In the water, an invisibility cloak, aka the mirage effect, was pretty handy.

Once he had the gloves snapped on, he quickly loaded up his backpack and filled his pockets with the rest of what he needed. With his phone tucked into the chest pocket, he looked at Diesel. He was fully outfitted as well. With a quick nod, Shane said, "We'll have to wipe out everything in the hallway."

"I've got that," said the MI6 operative, standing off to the side. "Gimme twenty seconds."

It was as late as they could leave and still hit their timeline. It was only ten p.m., but, as Shane opened the door, the lights in the hallway went out. The operative said, "You've got just ten minutes to get down to the bottom." And, with that, Shane and Diesel booked it. As soon as the door closed behind them, they raced down and out.

It wasn't long before they followed the pathway into the world beneath the street. The world of deliveries, the world of sewers, the world of underground trains. A world that most people didn't deal with. But a whole subset of the population reveled down here.

Shane might need some of their help, but what he definitely needed was a pathway to the building in question. They had all the intel they needed, at least he hoped so. He knew it wouldn't be as smooth as it could be because nobody had final answers for what the scenario would look like. He might have to come back, rethink the plan. But, more than that, he might have to request more gear to be delivered down here. MI6 was involved, and they would have somebody waiting topside at one of the turnstiles.

That was the agreement. He'd uphold it. He still didn't like it, but business was business. As he came around another corner in the underground tunnel, he held up a hand, as somebody was in front of them, his back to them. Shane quickly checked his phone to see a text message from MI6.

You're almost there. Two hundred yards ahead is our man.

Sending a message back, Shane typed, **We're already there.** He walked forward ever-so-slowly. The operative straightened, turned and looked at him, nodded and picked up the pace. They fell into step behind him, not a word spoken. As they raced underground toward the building in question, Shane could only hope that Shelly would understand, when she woke up and realized he wasn't there, that he couldn't stick around. They had a tight schedule as it was.

It wasn't the time or the place for that kind of goodbye, but he hoped that she knew that he would miss her no matter what. He could only hope he would make it back again. But he would do what he had to just to save her, just as he would to save his sister and the rest of her family. The fact that Shane had had his chain yanked by this asshole just made him even madder. On the other hand, the rage kept his footsteps moving in a steady beat underground.

When the operative finally came to a stop, he pointed up ahead, and, in a low voice, he said, "One hundred yards up, take a left," he said. "Then ten more yards and you're right beneath it."

"Got it." They moved past him without anything else being said. Shane didn't know if the agent would try to follow them and insert himself into their operation or if he would just keep an eye on them as they went. As soon as they got around the corner and up ahead, Diesel closed the gap between them and said, "He put a tracker on your back."

"Of course he did," Shane said, in a sarcastic tone. "What the hell? But I guess I'd rather have a tracker than actually have them on our tail. We'll leave it for now. If we drop it too quickly, they'll come ruin the operation."

"I guess that's what *cooperation* stands for these days," Diesel said.

"Hey, as hard we had to argue to avoid getting a whole team of theirs involved," he said, "we'll take what we can get."

"Still sucks though."

"Yep, it does. But let's go rescue this woman and see if we can get our asses home again."

"Yeah, that'll be the next problem," he said.

"What sucks is that we're open for all kinds of different problems, but we won't know what they are until we get there." And, with that, his footsteps slowed. They were at the marker that they had been directed to. They had passed through several steel doors into train passages, through sewers, and now they were literally standing at a ladder to a manhole that would lead them to the surface. But it would take them outside the building. Shane wanted to remain underground a bit farther.

Checking his GPS as he moved forward, he said, "So this is it. The outside of the building where she is. Now we have to find a way up from here."

"Well, the sewer's here," he said, "but it's all piped."

"I know," he said. He moved forward as the schematic showed and said, "This heads into the loading bay."

"And that's where the wall's the thinnest," Diesel said. "We could take a surface route and go into the loading bay from that direction, but there are cameras," he said.

"We could drill from underneath."

"Maybe," he said. "I was thinking of a hot torch, but getting through all that concrete will be rough."

"We have what we need, even C-4, which will give us a small *pop*, and completely weaken that area. But it'll go sideways," Shane said, "so no structural damage."

"Well, there'll be some," Diesel said, with a nod, "but it won't bring down the building."

"Still not sure it's the answer though." They had climbed up one level, so they were sitting at what should be on the other side of the loading bay. "Look at this," Shane said, scuffing his feet in some debris. "It's concrete, but it's crumbling." He made a fist and pounded into the concrete wall off to the side, watching more powder fall to the ground.

"Too much water in the mix," Diesel said, "or the wall was repaired."

"Either way, it's likely to be the weakest spot." They quickly checked the rest of it, then, with that decision made, they set up C-4, intended to blast the smallest hole that would do the job into the side wall, preferably not even going all the way through because they didn't want to announce their arrival just yet. They moved back and waited for the charge to go off.

Boom!

"That wasn't too bad," Shane muttered, as he quickly moved forward. It had definitely weakened the wall and even taken it all the way out in one spot. Using his hand, he pulled back the broken concrete and cleared a spot to see through. The room on the other side was dark. "No lights on here," he said. "We need to get through this as fast as we can." Pulling out a small sledge hammer he had brought along, he cracked down on the last of the concrete obscuring their way and climbed through headfirst.

As he slid to the other side, he realized the drop was a

little farther than he thought. They were actually higher up. That would work well for hiding the hole but made getting back up here much more of a hardship. He studied it for a long moment, then gave the all clear for Diesel to come through. As he did, Shane said, "Set your grappling hooks before you drop, so we can get out of here. It's higher than I expected."

They left lines coiled up in the hole that they should knock down a bit more in order to get back up and out again. They used their flashlights and quickly checked out the area. They were in a loading bay, with huge garage doors on the left. Boxes, forklifts, crates, pallets, and all the usual materials were on the right and in front of them. Keeping close to the perimeter, they maneuvered all the way to the innermost wall and to the first interior door.

According to the schematics they had accessed, this should be a way into the main lower level. The door was locked, but they took care of that easily. Less than two minutes later they were already deeper inside. They stopped because this area wasn't shown on the schematic. It was more hallways and small rooms. According to the schematic it should have been one big room, storage for all the material on the inside. But considering they had accessed a small door, they should have realized something was amiss. *Modifications done after the sale*, Shane thought.

They forged ahead, checking room after room. Nobody appeared to be in the building. This area was dark. Yet they weren't seeing any security cameras on the floor at all. But, then again, it was one of the lower levels, and often no security was down here anyway. Separating, they quickly searched the entire downstairs and found nothing. Both of them frowned, as they joined up again, and took the stairs up to the next floor. This was slightly below ground level, with half the windows at ground height. They went through this floor and again found nothing, no sign of anybody or even that the building had been occupied in a long time.

With his heart sinking, afraid that their intel had been bad, Shane and Diesel made their way up to the next floor. Here were at least signs of humans. This was the first floor aboveground, and they approached cautiously. Nobody was at the reception area, nobody in the hallway or around the elevators. Shane tilted his head, putting up a fist to stop Diesel from rushing forward.

With the two of them listening, they moved forward quietly. As they came up to an open doorway, they saw two apparent guardsmen, sitting, drinking coffee, with a TV show playing on the desk in front of them.

As one of the men got up to refill his coffee, the other one twisted around in his chair, his back to them. Shane and Diesel took advantage of that opportunity and dashed by the doorway and headed down the hallway to see just what these guards were supposedly guarding.

As Shane and Diesel came to the first room, they found a bunch of supplies—including bags, boxes, and some duffel bags with weapons, but no sign of the woman.

They headed to the next room, and this one was locked. Shane quickly unlocked it, and, with a quick dash, the two entered with guns ready. This looked like a small apartment and was more like what Shane expected. Especially considering the woman had been here for six months. As they went inside, they locked the door and quickly scanned through what appeared to be a living room and kitchen. When they came to another room, he saw a woman sleeping. He motioned to Diesel, and, keeping the lights off, he walked in and checked that she wasn't under guard. Slipping to the side of the bed, he immediately clasped a hand over her mouth. She woke with a jerk, and she stared at him in horror. As she tried to fight, he eased down and whispered, "We're here to rescue you."

She stared at him, sagging back in the bed, and then he discovered one more complication they didn't need. From the size of her belly, she was at least seven months' pregnant, maybe even full-term. He looked to Diesel to see him staring at this new development himself. The last thing they needed was a woman who couldn't move, at least not quickly, and she certainly couldn't climb, like they needed her to, for the hole they'd blown through. He sighed, helping her sit up, and asked, "How far along are you?"

"Eight-plus months," she said. "Who are you?"

"We're both Americans," he said. "Your father sent us."

She stared at him in shock. "Are you sure?" she asked.

He nodded. "Yes. Why?"

She shook her head. "Because it's been so long, I didn't think he cared."

"Well, he's been trying to get somebody to do the job."

"And that's you, I suppose."

Her voice was calm, as if she'd already thought through the worst that could happen and had made her peace with it. "How long have you been here?"

"Here in this place? A couple months," she said. "I was moved from another location. Actually it was a ship. I was kept for a long time in a small room. Then they brought me here. I think it was just too hard for them to look after me."

"And who is your father?"

She named the same guy they'd been dealing with. He nodded. "Yes, that's who arranged this."

"You don't appear to be very happy about it."

"I'm not. He kidnapped a close friend of mine and wiped out her entire department as a test to see if I could rescue her well enough that he would trust me to rescue you," he said in a hard voice. "Now he currently has my sister, her husband, and her children, all held hostage while I rescue you."

She gasped in horror, and then she shuddered, her eyes closed. "I'm so sorry," she said. "That's him. *Dear old Dad.*"

"Do you have much of a relationship with him?" he asked, as he helped her up, checking to see how mobile she was.

"I did at one time," she said, "but I planned to marry somebody he didn't approve of, and that set us back."

"And since then?"

"They killed my friend, when I was kidnapped," she said softly. "It doesn't matter what I feel about my father right now," she said. "If I can get out of this, save my child, avenge my friend, and get back to my fiancé," she said, "I'll be more than thankful for dear old Dad's assistance."

"Anybody else in your family?"

"No," she said, "just the two of us."

"Is he as bad as he appears?"

"Absolutely," she said. "He's a drug runner. A job I don't agree with. A career I tried to get him to stop, which was the end of our conversations for the longest time," she said. "But, at the moment, he has apparently come to my rescue, so I feel wrong saying anything negative about him."

"Families are complicated that way, aren't they?" he said.

She gave a brittle laugh. "What about the guards out there?" she asked. "Did you kill them?"

"No," he said, "I was hoping not to."

"You'll have to," she said. "The boss here will kill them anyway."

"Have you met him? Do you know what's going on?"

"He's trying to force my father to do something. I don't know what. But my father doesn't take kindly to people forcing him to do things," she said. "I'm just a pawn caught in the middle."

"Well, you're in England, in case you didn't know," he said, "and, with any luck, we can get you out of here."

"I hope it's not down to luck," she said. "I don't feel like my life has had any of that lately."

"Did these guys here kill your friend?"

"No. They are just hired guns. The man who kidnapped me is someone I know very well. He came to talk to me." She stopped speaking to collect herself.

"What happened?" Shane asked, as he went around the room and pulled out clothing for her. She just added the streetwear over her gown, dressing as quickly as she could in the darkness, given her condition.

"He came to talk to me. He wanted me to go with him. I refused. My friend stood up for me, and, before I knew it, they were in an argument. Just like that, my kidnapper pulled out a handgun and shot my friend in the head. The kidnapper didn't know I was pregnant," she murmured. "The bottom line is that he needed me to get my father to do something."

"Yeah," he said, "same as the friend of mine and the same as my sister. We're all just pawns, apparently." At that, he asked, "Do you have shoes?"

"Yes," she said, "but I can't put them on."

"Why not?" he asked, staring at her in confusion.

She smiled and said, "I can't reach my feet."

Diesel made a light snort, then quickly bent down, found her shoes, and slipped them on. After he'd tied them up firmly, he asked, "Is there anything here that you need?"

"No," she said, "I just need to get out of here safe and sound with my baby."

"The belly is bit of a complication we hadn't counted on," Shane admitted.

"Why is that?"

"I needed you to climb up a bit of a wall and exit through a hole, but I don't think it'll be big enough."

"Ah." She nodded.

"We'll just have to work around it," he said. "Are you ready to go?" She nodded. "Come on then. How mobile are you? Do you need any medication or anything like that?"

"No," she said, "and don't you worry about me being mobile," she said. "You show me a door out of here, and I'll make sure I'm out."

He nodded, and, leading her back toward the two guards, he held up a finger to his mouth and whispered, "The guards are in there, watching TV."

"They never come down my way anyhow."

"But we still have to get past their door," he said. She nodded. And although he'd locked the apartment behind them, he didn't trust that these guys wouldn't go check on her, even though she said that they didn't. What he really needed was to make sure that the guards had no clue what had happened. As he neared their break room and watched, one of the men got up and said, "What the hell happened to the popcorn anyway?"

"It's over in the cupboard," he said. "I told you that I moved it. We ran out of space."

"It's not a bad job, when you get to sit here and eat popcorn all evening," he said, patting his belly. "Although I'll get fat."

"You already are fat," the other guy said. That set the first man off in raucous laughter. He turned and started digging in the cupboard. "I can't see shit in here."

"I told you. It's down in the bottom."

He crouched at the bottom cabinet, and the second guy got up and joined him.

That was the movement they needed. With Diesel leading the way, and Shane taking up the rear, they quickly swept the pregnant woman across the open doorway. It occurred to Shane that he'd forgotten to ask for her name.

He heard the two men, still wrangling about popcorn behind them. After that, it was a simple case of leading the way back to the basement again. It was all too easy though. Something nagged Shane in the back of his mind, so he pulled up to Diesel and said, "I don't like this."

"Good," he said, "because neither do I."

The woman looked at them. "My name is Aleah, by the way, and what is it you don't like?"

"It's been far too easy. There was no need for all this preamble to this main event, if stealing you back was this simple."

"Well, I know a lot of the building is booby-trapped," she said. "So I think the point was to get us out without killing me."

"Booby-trapped how?"

"All the exits and the doors," she said, "even the windows."

"Which is fine since we entered through a wall," he said. "But getting you back out again? I don't know. I'm not so sure that's doable."

"I can climb," she said, a desperate note in her voice.

"I'm not sure you can," he said. Swearing to himself, he quickly retraced their steps back to the loading bay area, where they had first entered the building. He looked at it and said, "If we could even get out one of those doors …"

"Those are bound to be booby-trapped too," Diesel said.

Shane walked over with his flashlight, quickly checked, and swore. "Wires are everywhere here," he said.

"Like I said, booby-trapped," Aleah stated.

"And, once it sets off one, it'll set off the others." Shane turned to look at Diesel and asked, "Any ideas?" Diesel looked up at the hole that they had made, looked down at her, and said, "Nope," he said, "but we need to come up with something fast."

CHAPTER 8

S HELLY WOKE AND sat up with a start. A stranger was in the room, over by the table. She looked at the man in question and asked, "Who are you?"

"My name is Larry," he said quietly. "Shane and Diesel left me in charge."

"How are they?" she asked, pushing back the covers and realizing that somebody, likely Diesel, had thrown a blanket over the top of her.

"No word yet," he said.

She winced. "How long have they been gone?"

"Over three hours." He studied her quietly and said, "If you want, we can order up some coffee. If you think you can go back to sleep, that would be for the best."

"What time is it? Three o'clock in the morning?"

"After four actually," he said.

"When are they due back?"

"Anytime," he said. "That just means there are probably complications."

"Crap."

"One of the things that you learn about this business," he said, "is that there are always complications."

"So it's all about pivoting and adjusting as needed." She hopped up, went into the bathroom, and splashed some cold water on her face, wishing she would have woken up later.

But now that she knew, she didn't think there was any hope at all of her going back to sleep. As a matter of fact, as she checked her watch, it was a quarter to five. Back in the room, she sat down and said, "My name is Shelly. It's nice to meet you."

"Nice to meet you too," he said, with a ghost of a smile.

She studied that smile and said, "Shane warned you that I would be difficult, didn't he?"

"He said you might be a tad upset that they left without telling you."

"No, that's so typical of him," she said. "I just want him to get back safe again."

"We all do," he said.

"Any update on his family?" He shook his head, and she smiled. "Would you tell me if there was?" He shook his head again. She sighed. "You cloak-and-dagger guys are all the same."

"We all have responsibilities and duties, yes," he said. "If that makes us all the same, well, maybe so."

She sighed. "If you don't know anything, how will we know if something goes wrong?"

"When the news reports hit the TV," he said calmly.

She stared at him in shock. "Seriously?"

He shrugged. "Well, if the building blows up," he said, "there'll be a huge *boom*, and that's one way to get information," he said. "However, we're hoping that something subtler happens."

"A *boom*," she said faintly.

He nodded slowly. "The entire building is wired."

She sucked in a breath. "I know he does bomb squad and is some sort of an explosives expert."

"Sometimes it's just not worth the effort," he said.

"Meaning?"

"Meaning, sometimes it's wired and cross-wired, and they don't have time to figure it out. It doesn't matter how much skill you have if it's just too big of a job to manage in too short of an amount of time."

"So then what?" she asked. She hopped to her feet and paced. "He shouldn't even be over here in the first place."

"Nope, and you can bet an awful lot of us are out there, keeping an eye on what's going on, looking for whoever's behind this."

"Well, that would be nice," she said, "but, if the kidnapper's been smart enough to keep her six months without the father having a chance to get her, it won't be that simple."

"They likely moved her around," he said.

"That's still no excuse," she snapped.

"No, it might not have been," he said, with a laugh, "but that's often how it is."

"Still ugly," she said.

"No argument there," he said. "So what's the decision on coffee?"

"Coffee would be good," she said, with a sigh, as she settled down to wait.

"WE'LL HAVE TO go out one of the doors," Shane said.

"Then we're all dead," Aleah said.

He looked at her, shook his head, and walked to the door he had been examining. He checked out the big loading doors and the side doors. He figured the bay doors would be the easiest because they were huge. And any charges would likely have been run down along the ground. Of course, he'd seen them at the bottom of the bay doors, which should be better than wiring at the top of the bay doors, but he couldn't tell where any of the triggers were and just how badly this would blow.

He really liked the idea of blowing up this building though. He knew that it wasn't fair to the two guards inside, but, hell, they'd held a woman captive for all this time anyway. As it was, it would give Shane and Diesel a little bit of time to get her safely away. He looked at Diesel, smiled, and said, "You thinking what I'm thinking?"

"Probably not," Diesel said easily, "but I'm up for it anyway." Just then they heard ... "Shit! I think the alarm's gone off." And, sure enough, an alarm sounded through the building.

"We've got to go," Shane said. He looked down at the wires, shook his head, and said, "Aleah, I want you to head to the far corner. I'm setting the counterblast here along the doors," he said. "So, once the first blast goes, the entire building'll go. We'll have like three minutes to get out of here."

"*Great*," she said. "Are you sure there's no other option?"

"Not in the time frame we've got," he said, "unless you want to get locked up again."

"No, this is the farthest I've ever gotten," she said, "so I trust you. You've made it here."

"And I'm making it out of here too, with you and Diesel," he said. He quickly pulled the C-4 from his bag and set up the backfuse. As soon as it blew, he was already well out of range. He had deliberately chosen the wall that supported the garage door instead of the doors themselves. The corner of the wall blew, and he immediately saw the other charges, racing to light and explode. But Diesel was already there, urging Aleah forward.

Kicking out the remaining rocks, Shane got them both outside, and then the gunfire started. He took one in the bulletproof vest, and a second one slammed into the wall beside him. He then heard the charges going off inside the building. Aleah was behind him, tucked behind the stairs, even as the bullets flew, but they came from a single shooter. With Diesel racing off to the side, and Shane taking cover, they were in a showdown.

"What will you do now?" the gunman yelled. "I don't know who the hell you are," he said, "but you entered a game where you didn't belong."

Shane stayed quiet, as he studied the scenario. Diesel came up behind somebody else off to the side, just loading up a weapon, and took him out. *Good,* Shane thought to himself. *One down.* Diesel moved quickly around to the back of the shooter, and Shane called out to the gunman. "Show yourself. Surely you're not so weak and pathetic you just kidnap women and keep them hidden away like that," he said.

"You don't know anything about it," the guy said in a bored voice.

"Nope, and I don't really care to either," he said. And he stood up.

Immediately the guy raised his hand. "I want her over here."

"Yep, that makes sense to me," he said. He reached down and held out a hand. She looked at him and shook her head. He nodded. "Trust me," he whispered, then held her slightly behind him, as he twisted around to help her up. Bent over as he was, he fired one shot in the shooter's leg. The guy swore and dropped to his knees. Diesel was immediately on him, holding a gun to his head.

At that, Shane pulled Aleah to her feet and said, "Come on. Let's go see if this is the one we're looking for."

She hobbled with him closer to the gunman. She shook her head. "This is his assistant. He's not the one we need."

"Fine," he said, "but we'll take this one anyway." Just then the blast behind them in the building rippled out into the night. Shane was flung down. The gunman rolled to shoot Diesel, who popped him.

Two down. At that, Shane was immediately back on his feet. He looked to see Aleah on her knees, holding her belly. He bent down, scooped her up into his arms and ran.

"I think the baby's coming," she said.

"Well, you better tell Baby to hold up a bit," he said, "because that would be really shitty timing."

"I don't think babies care," she said and moaned.

Diesel was ahead of them, heading for the vehicle. It had been prearranged, but that didn't mean it was still lined up. As soon as Shane saw Diesel get into it and drive toward him, Shane swore and said, "Thank God for that." Shane scooted inside the back seat, gently setting Aleah down, staying with her.

Diesel looked up in the rearview mirror and asked, "Hospital?"

He shook his head. "No, that'll just get more people killed. Head to the docks."

"And what about Shelly?"

"I'll send her a message." He quickly texted her. **We're out. We have the woman. She's heavily pregnant. Heading to Dock 41 to load up. Stay safe.**

She wrote back immediately. **I don't know about the *stay safe* part, but I have to tell you. Things just changed.**

CHAPTER 9

S HELLY STARED AT the MI6 agent, now holding a gun on her. "What did I do to you?"

He shrugged. "You're just in the wrong place at the wrong time."

"You know what? I'm getting really damn tired of people telling me that," she cried out. "You said that, when the bombs went off, you would know what had happened. So tell me. What has happened?"

"It means he failed," he said. "And that means I need to take you as a hostage."

"Why?" she asked, staring at him. Then it hit her. "Of course. You're not working for MI6. You're working for the other guys."

"I've been working for both for a long time," he said. "Sometimes you have to do what you have to do, just to stay alive."

"So you're a double agent," she said. "Jesus. Only me. Only in my world could things get so messed up."

He smiled and said, "It is what it is. Now let's go."

"Where are we going?"

"To the docks," he said. "We'll meet at the rendezvous area."

"What's the point of that?" she asked.

"I have to make sure that they didn't get out somehow,"

he said. "If they did, and she's there, I have to recapture her."

She stared at him. "So that was all part of the plan? Wait for Shane to see if he succeeded? If he did, grab her again, squeeze her father down a little bit more, take out everybody involved, and then walk away?"

"I've been trying to walk away from this nightmare for a long time," he said. "This is the perfect opportunity."

"Unbelievable," she said.

"Now," he said, "grab your bag and let's go." She picked up her bag, still swearing, when her phone vibrated slightly. She looked at him and asked, "Can I go to the bathroom?"

"Yes, but don't close the door." She rolled her eyes at that, then walked in quickly, used the bathroom, then trying to send a quick message. But even as she typed it, the phone was ripped out of her hand.

"That'll be your last freebie," he said calmly.

She glared at him. "And what? You'll just kill me?"

"Absolutely," he said. "I should have popped you before, just to make sure that you wouldn't be a problem, but I know he wants leverage, so this is my answer."

"Great," she said, swearing. But now that she didn't have a phone, she couldn't send the needed intel to Shane. "Let's go see who won the battle, your guy or my guy," she said. "Hands down, I'm saying my guy."

"Good," he said. "Then I can take everybody I need and get out of this."

"You'll never get out of it," she said. "You're in too deep."

"Which is why I'm working so hard to get out," he said. "Sometimes things just snowball." He led her away, the gun in his pocket, smiling at the early morning staff, as he took her down to the basement of the hotel.

"What if I cry out?" she asked, in a conversational voice. "I mean, just out of curiosity."

"Well, whatever attention you attract," he said, "that's fine. I'll just have to kill them too." At that, she fell silent because she knew instinctively that he would. "Were you involved in the shooting in New York?"

"No, of course not," he said. "I wouldn't dirty my hands with that. That was another team entirely."

"Oh, I see. So there's honor among thieves. You only kill when you need to?"

"Something like that," he said. "I wouldn't worry about it though. This won't be your day."

"Hasn't been my week yet," she said.

"Too bad lover boy didn't leave you back in New York," he said.

"We didn't think it was safe," she murmured.

"You know something? It probably wasn't, but it's not very safe for you here either."

She shook her head. "I don't think he thought it would be this bad."

"Well then, he didn't look at every contingency, did he?"

"No, I think he was trying to get along with MI6," she muttered, "but they just stabbed him in the back."

"I'll have to come up with a really good way to make sure my ass is covered."

"Sure. Like what?"

"I don't know. Maybe I'll convince them that you were a part of all this from the beginning." He gave her a smile that made her blood run cold, as she stared into his dead flat eyes.

THE TRIP WAS hard, fast, furious, and completely in darkness. Nobody inside made a sound. Even outside, driving with the lights off during a full moon, they slipped through the city and headed for the docks. Only as they arrived, the engine idling, staring around from the back seat, did Aleah ask, "Is it safe?"

He twisted to look at her, the pain evident in her face. "Yes," he said, "at the moment anyway. How are you doing?"

"It'll be hours yet," she said, her hands on her belly.

"You mean, you hope so."

She gave a broken laugh. "This is not how I intended to give birth," she said. "On the other hand, I'm not a captive all alone in that nasty-ass apartment," she said. "So, for that, I thank you very much."

"You're welcome," he said, "but we're far from done yet."

"I get it." She took a long slow deep breath, and he watched as the movement shifted up and down her body.

Shane looked at Diesel. "We need to get moving."

Diesel nodded. "I'll go ahead and scout things out," he said. "We should have a boat waiting. I'll give you the signal."

"Okay," Shane replied.

Diesel slipped out of the truck, closed the door with a nearly silent *click*, and disappeared from sight. With their bags ready, Shane opened up his side and carefully helped Aleah out of the back seat.

"How long until the next one?" he asked.

"Hopefully a long time," she said. "They're getting worse."

"I hear you," he said, "but hang on, until we can get you

on the ship."

She laughed. "You make it sound so easy."

"It's not easy at all," he said. "I get that. I've never been in this position, and I understand it's not easy on you." He smiled. "I'm just asking you to do what you can to help us get you there."

"I'll do anything I can to save my child," she said.

He hesitated, looked at her, and said, "I didn't ask, and nobody said, but who is the father?"

She smiled a gentle smile. "Renault. A good man," she said. "Hopefully he's waiting for me, but I have no idea."

"Does he know anything about this?"

"I don't know. He was in the military but was deployed before I was taken. I have no way of knowing what he knows and couldn't trust anything my captors would tell me anyway."

"Would your father have told him?"

"Never. He didn't approve."

"Got it," he said, "but that doesn't mean that Renault's still not the best man for you."

"I would take him in a heartbeat, if I could," she said. "He's one of the most honorable men I know, which puts him in a completely different class from all the men my father associates with."

"And your father himself."

"As bad as any of them, worse perhaps," she admitted softly. "It's not an easy time right now."

"No, it isn't," he said. "I do believe he's been trying to get somebody to get you out of here though."

"I'm sure he has," she said.

In the distance he heard one long whistle followed by two short ones. He motioned to her and asked, "Can you walk?"

"Yes, I can walk," she said. "Just show me to where."
Together, they moved slowly but steadily toward Diesel.

They were almost there at the dock, when Shane caught
sight of a flash. He immediately threw himself down to the
ground, taking her with him—Shane hitting the dock, her
landing on him, protecting her. He felt a pull on his shoulder, then rolled, jumped to his feet, snatched her up into his
arms, carrying her, and raced down the dock.

Diesel was already at the edge of the dock, firing into the
darkness. But, with every shot he fired, his position was
revealed as well. Shane handed Aleah off to Diesel, snatched
his handgun from his holster, and gave covering fire to make
sure that the two of them got as far as they could down the
dock. He heard the idling of a motor. *Good.*

In the distance he heard a man call out, "Stop. I have
your girlfriend."

Shane froze. He crouched down deep at a piling.

The man called out again, "Equal trade."

Shane closed his eyes because no way he could do that.
Two lives were being put into a Zodiac right now, three,
counting Baby, yet no way he could let Shelly be forsaken.

Sure enough, she called out, "I'm fine. Just go."

He shook his head, feeling the weight of the world on
his heart. But he already heard the Zodiac idling gently in
the water. "You're too late," he called out. "I can't stop it
now."

"Well, I can," the gunman said, and gunfire sounded in
Shane's direction, hard and heavy, more of a spray tactic for
Shane's benefit than actually directed at him. But it was
effective at keeping him in place. As soon as it stopped,
Shane slipped behind a storage bin a good twenty feet to his

right. More shots were fired, but he had gained a bigger barrier for the ongoing gunfire. He didn't know if Diesel had taken off with Aleah or not, but Shane hoped so for her sake.

When he heard a footstep behind him, he turned, his gun ready, to see Diesel with his finger to his lips, whispering at him, "I'm going right," he said. "Cover me."

Instantly Diesel raced around the corner, heading toward the far side, as Shane stepped up with as much gunfire as he could and pummeled it in the direction where the earlier shots had come from. He knew he was in danger of hitting Shelly, and that was something he hoped to God that he would never have to live with. He aimed above five feet, still hoping to God she was down on the ground and safe somewhere. He heard a cackle of laughter in the distance.

"Missed me," he said. "You'll hear from me soon." And, with that, an engine fired up and took off.

Both Shane and Diesel raced into the darkness after the vehicle, shooting at it, its lights on as it headed off. Shane had his phone out, already calling Gavin, setting up tracking. At the same time, he contacted the military, looking to close off all land exits from the docks. They kept running behind the vehicle, hoping they could get at least a roadblock set up right away. The vehicle suddenly swerved to one side and then the other, wildly shifting as they watched, as if the driver were fighting with somebody.

Diesel said, "Uh …"

"Shit," Shane said, picking up speed and racing toward the vehicle, which still slipped from the right to the left and then back over again.

"She's doing it again, isn't she?" Diesel asked, as they ran.

"Yes," he said in frustration.

"Well, I'm not sure if it's good or bad, but, damn it, she's likely to get herself shot."

Just then a shot rang out, and the vehicle slowly rolled to a stop. They raced up behind it, immediately opened the doors, and shoved their guns into the front seat, calling out, "Hands up!"

And there was Shelly, her face white, yet still wired, her eyes red and bloodshot. She stared at Shane, her breathing raspy. "I didn't mean to kill him," she cried out.

He looked at her in shock, reached down, and placed a finger against the gunman's neck. Sure enough, he was dead. Shane looked at the position of his body and realized, when the guy tried to fire at her, she'd jumped on him, twisting his wrist around. Because of the small confines of the truck, he had pulled the trigger, shooting himself. He shook his head. "Come on out," he said.

She immediately scrambled out the passenger side, and Shane snatched her up into his arms and just held her tight.

"Where's the woman?" she asked, pulling back and looking up at him.

"She's headed out to the destroyer." He noted the blood all over her. He just hoped it wasn't hers.

"Good. It's been a pretty rough day. Can I join her?" she asked, shivering.

"That's actually not a bad idea." He looked at Diesel, studying her too, nodding. "Maybe we can get the Zodiac back." Shane stepped away and made a quick call. Instead a helicopter lifted off the destroyer a few minutes later and soon landed in front of them, and Shelly, bag in hand, was quickly loaded up to be taken out to the destroyer.

"I have to stay here, honey. Explain to the locals."

As she looked at him, she lifted a hand in goodbye. He

stood there for a long moment, staring, until the chopper took off.

"You should have told her that you love her, man," Diesel said, shaking his head, offering his romantic advice once more.

"She knows," Shane replied, focused on the helicopter as it carried her away.

"Sure, but she doesn't know in a way that counts," he said. "She knows that you love her, but not *love her*-love her."

Shane glared at his friend in irritation and got a cheeky grin back. Shane just groaned, then shook his head. "Not to change the subject, but what the hell is going on here?"

"Well," Diesel said, "I would guess that this guy she shot is a double agent—in this case, one who had managed to operate within MI6."

Very quickly they were surrounded by police, as the pier suddenly filled with vehicles. MI6 was here as well. They quickly walked over, and it took Shane only moments to explain the gunfire, sharing what they had seen and done and the little bit that Shelly had told him. The evidence in the vehicle supported her account. MI6 had grim expressions on their faces and remained quiet as they dealt with the scenario, including the traitorous member of their force who lay dead in the vehicle.

They looked at Shane and said, "Go on out to the destroyer. We'll handle this."

"Love to," he said. He and Diesel eased out of the fray, just as the media appeared, which served to spur them on to race down to the end of the pier. Hoping to find a ride for themselves, they found a Zodiac but no attendant. They hopped in, turned on the engine, and quietly slipped away toward the destroyer. They sent a message ahead, so they would be expected.

Shortly thereafter, they climbed up the ship and, for the first time in a long while, stood safely on board.

CHAPTER 10

THE HELICOPTER LANDED in the darkness, its lights shining, eerie glows all around. Then more noise, more men, and more lights—red and white, some flashing—together, it all overwhelmed her senses. Shelly had gone from being a kidnap victim, for the second time, to fighting for and gaining her freedom, then being rushed onto a helicopter and brought on board this huge naval ship.

Even now she was escorted quickly to a completely different area of the ship. As she entered the double doors, she realized she'd been taken to the medical center. A woman immediately greeted her and took her into another small room, where she was stripped down, given a hospital gown, and asked to sit on a bed.

None of her protests had worked. "I'm fine, you know?" she said. "I just have a bit of a headache is all."

The woman nodded and said, "A doctor will check you over in a few minutes."

Shelly realized there was no point in arguing. She would be checked over, whether she agreed to be or not. And maybe that was for the best, considering her headache just got worse and worse. She lay here quietly, dozing and then jerking awake, and she realized maybe things could start to return to normal now. Whatever that meant.

She could only hope that Shane was okay. And Diesel.

She knew better than to actually shake her head, so she just mentally shook it at the thought. Of course Shane and Diesel were okay because everything was already over, right? She shivered, pulling the sheet tight up around her neck.

When a man in a white lab coat walked in, he took one look and made a startled exclamation, then disappeared and quickly returned with a warm blanket that he wrapped around her. It was so warm and cozy, she moaned in relief. "I'm sorry," he said. "I've been delayed by another new patient."

"That's fine," she whispered. "Are you the doctor? Is the pregnant woman okay?"

"She's in labor, and we're likely to have a child within a couple hours," he said with a smile.

"Will she be all right?"

"Well, I don't know the full story," he said, "but she's in good hands now."

Shelly smiled up at him. "It must have been a while since you were in a maternity ward, delivering babies."

He broke out into a low chuckle. "You're right about that," he said, "but I've delivered plenty. I must admit that everybody on board is pretty excited."

She smiled and snuggled deeper into the blanket. "I'm glad she's okay. She's been to hell and back."

"Doesn't sound like you've had an easy time of it by any means yourself," he replied. "Again, I don't have the full story, but I'll need to check you over."

She yawned and said, "I'm fine, you know?"

"I'm glad to hear that," he said gently. "In that case, you won't have a problem with me checking you over."

She groaned and said, "What do you need?"

"Just roll over on your back," he said gently. And, with

that, he did a thorough exam, including her pulse, blood pressure, and listening to her heart and lungs. She lay here quietly, letting him do his thing. When he was done, she said, "See? I told you that I'm healthy."

He looked at her, smiled, and said, "Yeah, so let's take a look at that head."

"What's wrong with my head?" she said, opening her eyes wider. "I've got one heck of a headache, so I think I must have bumped it."

"You think so, huh?" He gently parted her hair, and she cried out. "Yep," he said. "Just as I thought. We'll need to stitch this."

"Stitches? Did I cut it?"

"Something like that," he said in a noncommittal voice.

She said, "I'm really tired."

"I'll need you to stay awake a little bit longer," he said.

"I don't want to," she said in a cranky tone. "My head hurts. I told the nurse about it earlier."

"Yes, you did," he said, "and that's good. Sit tight. I just need to grab a few things, and then we'll take care of the head."

"Stitches, you said."

"Yep, definitely stitches," he said.

She realized at some point that somebody else had joined him. They spoke in low tones, but she was starting to doze off again. The nurse suddenly reached over and gave Shelly a gentle shake that just hurt her head even more. She opened her eyes, glaring through the pain, snapping, "Don't do that. It hurts."

"I get that," she said, "but I need you awake."

"Wait. Am I hurt worse than I thought I was?"

At that, the nurse chuckled. "We already knew you had a

headache," she said, "and you've heard the doctor say you need stitches."

"Yeah, but stitches don't sound so bad."

"No, but it looks like you've got quite a bullet burn alongside your head," she said.

Shelly looked at her in shock. "Bullet? Wait. What? But not inside though, right?"

"Nope. It skated along the surface of your head, so it looks like you've had a very lucky escape, but it'll cause you quite the headache for a while."

"*Lucky escape*, yeah, you could say that. Kidnapped twice and a bullet skimming my head," she said, yawning. "It's been a hell of a week." She immediately tried to close her eyes again.

"No, ma'am, open those eyes, please," ordered the nurse in a firm voice.

Shelly opened her eyes and glared at her. "Pretty soon you won't stop me," she snapped. "I'll just collapse."

"The doctor will be back in just a minute."

"I'm too tired," she said. "Can't you just give me some anesthetic, so I can sleep while you do it?"

"It'll be a local," the nurse said in a firm voice, "and we'll need you to stay awake."

"Why?" she asked.

"Because we don't know how severe the damage is yet."

"It'll hurt, won't it?" she said, biting her lip.

The woman looked down at her, with a smile, and said, "Surely somebody who's survived being kidnapped twice in one week can handle a few stitches."

She glared at her. "That was a cheap shot."

The nurse chuckled. "You're right. It was," she said, "but it worked. You have a temper, and it looks like it'll be enough to keep you going."

A soft chuckle came from inside the room. "Not only has she got a temper but she tends to let it out at very interesting times."

Shelly recognized his voice at once and cried out, "Shane!" Instantly she grimaced in pain. Yet she relaxed when he gripped her hand in his firm grasp and kissed her gently on the cheek.

"What are you doing in here?" he asked.

"You put me here," she said, aggrieved. "If I was at home, I could have taken care of this myself and been sleeping right now."

"I don't think so," he said, after a moment. "You need stitches, I hear."

"They'll cut my hair, won't they?" she said sadly.

He burst out laughing. "If that's the only thing wrong here," he said, "I think you'll survive." He looked at the nurse. "How bad is it?"

"Bad enough," she said in a low tone.

He said, "I'd like to take a closer look, but I don't want to hurt her."

"Don't touch it," Shelly said immediately.

Just then the doctor returned. "We'll take her into the OR and do this."

"What?" she said, trying to sit up and to get out of bed. Only then her view of the room got woozy. She looked up at Shane and said, "Uh-oh," and fainted.

"THAT'S MY GIRL," Shane said, with a smile. "Can we get her done before she wakes up again?"

"We'll have to," the doctor said. "She didn't seem to be aware of the head injury, until we mentioned it to her. She just said she had a bit of a headache."

"She's always had a blind spot when it comes to pain. As long as she didn't look at a needle when going in, she was fine. The minute she saw the needle, she was out. If she didn't look at a cut, she was fine. The minute she looked at it and washed it, she would faint."

The doctor and nurse just smiled, nodded. The doc said, "Now, if you'll step outside,"—he pointed—"we'll go get her taken care of."

Shane took one last look, leaned over, kissed Shelly again, and said, "Take good care of her. She's had a hell of a week."

"Got it," the doctor said cheerfully. "She's in our hands now."

And, with that, Shane stepped outside the room, where Diesel waited for him.

"How is she?"

"Heading for surgery."

Diesel's expression showed his surprise. "I didn't realize she was hurt that bad."

"It's so hard with head injuries, since they bleed so much anyway," Shane said.

"We got her onto the ship really fast," Diesel said. "They'll do the best they can for her."

He nodded. "She's got a bullet burn running along her scalp. A bullet from my gun. I feel terrible about it."

"You don't know that for sure. We got her away," Diesel said. "Matter of fact, we got them both away."

"Speaking of which …" He turned and stepped to the one nurse sitting at her desk. "How's Aleah doing?"

She looked up. "Are you the father?"

"No," he said, "we rescued her."

"Ah," the nurse said. "She's a couple hours away from delivering."

"That long still?" he asked.

She nodded. "Unless things pick up quickly," she said, "but everything is on target."

"Well, that's good news. May I see her?" She hesitated, and he said, "I just want to know that she's okay. We went through a lot together."

She got up and said, "Just a minute and I'll check." She disappeared into another room.

He looked at Diesel. "It's kind of funny. You hand them over, and then you don't get to see them again."

"Nothing funny about it," Diesel said, with a wry smile. "It's damn frustrating."

The nurse came back. She had a smile on her face. "Aleah would like to see you."

"Me too?" asked Diesel.

"One at a time, please," she said.

"Deal."

Shane walked into the room to see Aleah stretched out on a bed, white sheets covering her massive belly, her arm hooked up to an IV, but a smile was on her face. He walked over and squeezed her hand and asked, "How are you doing?"

"Thanks to you," she said, "I'm fine."

"And Baby is making his appearance pretty soon, huh?"

"Well, I hope so," she said. "This would be a nice time to have my baby, when I'm safe and secure," she said. "Listen. Do not trust that you have this issue taken care of," she warned him.

"Meaning?" He sat down carefully on the edge of her bed and studied her face.

"He's not done," she added. "He'll come back after you."

"And you too?"

"I hope not," she said. "With the doctor's help, I've already sent word to my father that I'm free," she said. "I hope, with that, he can turn around and take care of this problem, so I don't have to keep looking over my shoulder."

"Wouldn't that be nice," he said. "I've also told my team that you're out and safe," he said.

"There was a lot of commotion here about another woman," she said. "What was that all about?"

"My friend was taken prisoner in New York earlier this week, courtesy of your father. I brought her with me to London to keep her safe, but one of the MI6 agents turned out to be a double agent and was helping the same guy who kidnapped you. So, when I took you to the dock," he said, "I found out that the agent had kidnapped my friend and was at the dock also, looking to make an exchange, right after we had sent you off in the Zodiac."

"Oh, so that's what it was all about," she said. She tossed her head from side to side. "God, this nightmare just doesn't stop."

"Well, I've got my friend back. She's in surgery right now," he said, "but we have to reassess and figure out what we'll do to put a stop to this permanently."

She opened her eyes, looked at him "You'll have to take him out," she said. "I'm not one to advocate murder," she added, "but he'll never stop."

"Who? Your father? Or your kidnapper?"

"Both." Her expression was grim but determined.

"Well, your father now has my sister and her family," he said. "We're waiting for contact, so we can make a trade, but we're getting mixed signals on who is calling the shots."

"Shit," she said, staring up at him in horror.

He shook his head. "No, we won't hand you over," he said, "to your father or anyone else, but we will get my family back."

"Do you think it'll be … do you know they're still okay?"

"Well, I certainly hope so," he said. "There won't be a good end to this for anybody who harms them."

"Meaning, you'll run him down?"

"I'll run him down and take him out, whether it's your father or your kidnapper," he said, his voice hard. "Nobody gets to do something like that."

"I'm sorry," she whispered. "I know your family is important to you, but this guy—my kidnapper—has absolutely no conscience. He wants my father to do something, and he won't stop until it's done, and it's clear that my father won't buckle."

"He especially won't buckle now," Shane said, "now that he knows that you're free."

She turned her head to the side and said, "I'm so sorry."

"Don't," he said. "We're working on it right now."

"Please don't hand me over," she said again, her voice shaking with fear.

He reached down and gripped her hands and said, "We won't. You have my word on that."

She sagged in place. "Thank you," she said. "I feel safe right now. I just don't know where to go from here."

"None of us do at the moment," he said, "but we'll figure it out."

CHAPTER 11

PAIN WOKE UP Shelly first, and yet it was a building pain, almost like a hammer inside her head that kept her awake. She lay here, hot tears running down her cheeks, feeling weak, just wanting to go home and to be done with this. When someone gently stroked her hand and said, "We're upping the pain medication," Shelly let herself sink back under with relief.

She wanted to tell them to raise it up so high that she was put out permanently. The pain was that bad. On the other hand, when she woke the second time, maybe the drugs were working better because she wasn't quite so badly in agony. She surfaced a third time, realizing that the room was dark, and it was either the next day or late that evening. She was completely out of sync with the world around her.

When she shifted in the bed and tried to sit up, immediately the door opened, and a woman walked in.

"What can I do for you?"

"I need to go to the bathroom."

"Actually you have a catheter in."

She frowned, sagging back onto the bed. She hadn't even noticed. "I really don't like those."

"Maybe not," she said, "but you don't need to physically go to the bathroom then."

Shelly sighed gently to avoid any pain. "Well, I thought

I needed to," she said, shaking her head. "Ow," she said, reaching to hold her head.

"Sorry about that," the nurse said cheerfully. "If you can go back to sleep one more time," she said, "when you wake up in the morning, we can take out the catheter. Then you can get up and maybe have a shower."

"The magic word," Shelly said and stared at the woman with hope in her eyes. "Am I that much better?"

"It wasn't too, too bad," she said, "but you need to give it a chance to heal a bit."

"Fine," she murmured, yawning deeply. "Until next time." And, with that, she sank back into sleep.

When she woke up the next time, it was morning. She saw people moving around the facility through the glass panels separating her room from the others. She took a long slow deep breath, realizing that she didn't feel too terribly bad, as long as she didn't move too much.

The door opened almost immediately, and the doctor stepped in. "There's my patient," he said, with a bright smile. "How are you doing?"

She looked up at him. "Outside of the headache?" she asked. "I'm fine. I woke up several times in the night from the pain, but I'm feeling much better now."

"Good," he said. "Let me check your head." He did a thorough exam and then continued, "If you feel up to it, and, as long as you have somebody to help you, a shower would make you feel a lot better. Then we can get you back into bed, where you'll stay for at least the rest of the day. I'll want to take a look at that head wound again tonight."

She grinned. As he walked out, she asked, "Does that mean I can get rid of this catheter?"

"Yep, absolutely," he said. He disappeared, and a nurse

came back in and very quickly removed the catheter and helped her to slowly stand up.

"See if you can walk a step or two," she said. "That'll determine how much help we'll need to give you for your shower."

Shelly got up, slowly walked around the bed, into the bathroom, took one look at her face in the mirror, and winced. "Well, I can walk," she said, "but I look pretty scary."

The nurse chuckled. "I don't know about that," she said. "That boyfriend of yours has been in here almost constantly. As much as we would let him, at least," she admitted. "He didn't think you looked pretty scary at all."

Shelly smiled at that. "Shane's just a friend," she said, "but we've always been close."

"I don't know about that *just a friend* part," she said. "That wasn't a *just a friend* look in his eyes."

"He probably feels guilty." But it made her heart feel good nonetheless.

"Says you, but I know what I saw," the nurse replied.

Shelly just chuckled, shrugged, and said, "He's a good man."

"I would agree," she said. "A good-looking one too."

"He is that. He's always got women trolling around him all the time."

"But not you?" the nurse asked, with curiosity.

"No, because we've been such good friends, it just wasn't anything that we particularly wanted to change."

"Hell, I would have hopped into bed with him in a heartbeat," she said with a laugh.

Shelly smiled. "But to hop in bed with him meant to lose him, and I didn't want to do that."

"You are a stronger woman than I am," she said with a smile. "So, how are you feeling about a shower at this point?"

"That would be awesome."

"If you need a hand, I'll be in here changing your bed."

With that, Shelly turned on the water and sat on the edge of the bench, until she was strong enough, and then used the rails and pulled herself up and just stood here, letting the hot water slide down her body. She hadn't realized just how much this last week had preyed on her. It had been a cycle of adrenaline rush and shock, over and over. And yet the only thing she could think of was the fact that Shane had apparently stayed here with her all night. But, if their positions had been reversed, she would have done the same.

She did love him; she always had. They'd never taken their relationship past that because they always had other relationships in their world. She wondered if they had deliberately avoided having something between them, but it was just way too confusing to sort out.

She did like the fact that he was here for her the whole time. And maybe that was the difference. Just the fact that they were older, and they were different, and maybe it was a better time for them to have a different sort of relationship. Anytime she thought about him, it was always with that warm, cozy feeling of somebody very special to her, and that had never changed. He was special. Always had been.

She smiled as she slowly worked some water over the stitches. She hadn't asked the nurse if she could get them wet, but neither had the nurse said anything about it.

Just then the nurse called out, "You okay?"

"Hard to shampoo," she said.

"Well, the stitches can get wet," she said. "Otherwise we

wouldn't have let you shower. Do you want a hand?"

With that, Shelly sat on the bench, and the nurse slowly and carefully massaged some shampoo in and around Shelly's head. Then she used the handheld showerhead and rinsed off her hair. They repeated it once more, the pain actually easing with the warm water.

When they were done, Shelly asked, "How do the stitches look?"

"Nice and clean," the nurse said. "Let me get a small towel, and we can pat that all down and then bundle up your hair and get the rest of you dressed."

And that's what they did. By the time Shelly wore a new hospital gown and was back in bed, she was shaky and teary. She'd only just gotten under the covers, when a knock came at the door.

"Come in," she said softly, hoping her head wouldn't hurt. A head poked around the corner. She smiled. "Hey, Shane. How are you?"

"I'm fine," he said. "The question really is, how are you?"

"Well, I just had a shower."

"How about a cup of coffee?" he said, waggling his eyebrows.

She stared at him. "You know how much I love you already," she said, "but if you bring me coffee …"

He nudged the door open wider with his shoulder and stepped in, holding two big mugs.

She cried out in delight and slowly shifted her position, so she leaned up against the headboard. She accepted a cup from him gratefully. "There's nothing quite like that first cup in the morning," she said, "particularly after a crappy night."

"How was your night?"

"I kept waking up from the pain," she admitted, "but the doctor says I'm doing fine."

"Perfect," he said.

"How long am I here for?"

"I'm not sure yet," he said. "We'll have to hear from the doctor first."

"Well, I can hardly sit here at the US Navy's expense," she said, "when I could go home to recuperate."

"It's a little more complicated than that," he said. "Until we actually capture this guy, you're still in danger."

She stared at him in shock and then sipped her coffee. Her mind raced, as she thought about the implications. "You know, if I still had a job," she said, "I would have lost it by now."

"Not necessarily," he murmured. "These are extenuating circumstances."

She groaned at that. "What about your sister?"

"No word yet," he said, his tone grim.

"They'll want to trade. You know that?"

"I know. In fact," he hesitated and then said, "the kidnapper just reached out."

"And?"

"They want Aleah in exchange for my family."

"So, two in exchange for four. That's hard too."

"Very," he said. "Of course her father has also reached out, with his utmost thanks, but now suddenly is getting cagey and denies having my sister. We can't rule him out of any of this mess either, since he's the one who has taken so many lives to get his daughter back already. The fact that Aleah wants nothing to do with him is telling as well."

"No happy ending for her in this, is there?"

"It's hard to see how," he said. "I'm not exactly sure what the answer is for any of us at the moment, but I will promise to keep you safe. You and Aleah and the baby."

She stared at him, knowing that he was making the promise to the best of his ability, but this scenario could be way past anything he could do. "I think we need to find the guy who kidnapped her," she said, "and figure out how to get your sister back safe from whoever the hell has Prissy and her family. Then, at some point, you'll have to deal with the father."

"I know," he said, "and I'm not looking forward to any of it, but—"

"But you will," she said gently, "because it's what you do."

He laughed. "It is what I do. I just hadn't expected it to become quite so personal."

"That's life," she said. She looked down at the coffee that was almost gone and asked, "Any chance of some food to go with this?"

"I can go to the kitchen and see," he said, hopping to his feet. "Finish that, and I'll bring you another one."

She beamed at him. "Thank you." And then she stopped and said, "Oh, my goodness. What about Aleah? How is she? What about the baby?"

His expression changed into a look of wonder. "She had a little girl this morning."

"Oh, that's wonderful," she said, then frowned. "I slept through that."

"Maybe that was one of the reasons you kept waking up," he said. "Maybe your subconscious was figuring that out."

"Have you seen her yet?"

"Not yet, she's asleep," he said. "I'll stop by after this."

"Well, go say hi to her and then see what you can rustle up for food and more coffee."

He nodded, leaned down, kissed her gently on the cheek, and said, "Stay safe."

"Am I in danger here?" she asked in a small voice.

He shook his head. "No."

"You realize that's what you said at the hotel too."

"Yeah, don't remind me. I'm really sorry about that. And don't worry. MI6 is pretty upset about the whole deal. They're scrambling right now, going through the cases that guy was on for the last ten, twenty years, wondering just how much damage he's caused."

"Can we find answers to some of the outstanding questions through investigating his life?"

"They're looking into it, and our guys are as well."

"Well, I hope so," she said. "I'm pretty well done with all this."

He looked at her, smiled, and said, "And what will you do when it's all over?"

"I have no clue," she said, "but it did occur to me that it's a gift in a way. I get a chance to reset my life and to figure out what I want to do and to make a decision. It might even help making my new life happen."

"In what way?"

"I wasn't really that happy in New York," she said. "I found it difficult to meet people. They weren't terribly friendly. It's superbusy, superfoggy, and I just wasn't that happy."

"So back to California?"

"Maybe," she said, "but to one of the smaller towns back off the coast."

"You tell me where," he said, "and I'll help you make it happen." And, with that, he disappeared.

She stared in his wake for a long moment. He'd always been a good friend, and she was just starting to realize that what they had was actually way past good friends. Maybe it had been a case of not the right time for them yet, but maybe it was now.

Shelly settled back in bed and smiled at the idea of a little baby girl being saved at the same time. And Shelly closed her eyes and dozed off to sleep once again.

SHANE WALKED TO the nurse, still carrying the two empty mugs, and asked, "Any chance I can see Aleah?"

"I'm not sure if she's awake yet," the nurse said, bouncing to her feet, "but let me check." She disappeared, in a much happier mood this time than the last time he had asked. She came back with a bright smile, so he figured he'd get the go-ahead.

"She's awake and would like to see you."

He expressed his thanks with a smile, then stepped into the room. "How's Momma?"

Aleah beamed at him. "Tired, worn out, and very happy to be a mom right now," she said. "I can't thank you enough for saving me. Us, I mean. For saving us."

"I'm glad that it all worked out okay," he said. "You sure scared me when you went into labor."

She burst out laughing. "Scared you?" she said. "After everything I'd already been through, believe me. That was the last thing I wanted."

"On the other hand," he said, "it sounds like your

daughter is healthy and doing very well."

"She is," she said, looking off to the side at the incubator. "I still can't believe it really. After everything, plus thinking I would have to deal with those men and give birth in captivity on my own ..." She shook her head and said, "This was definitely a much nicer experience and a welcome surprise." She hesitated, looked up at him, and asked, "And your friend?"

"They did surgery to close up the wound in her head," he said. "She's recovering a couple rooms over, but she'll be just fine. She was pretty lucky." Aleah beamed at the news. "However," he added, "there's no sign of the man who kidnapped you, and we've had a missive from him and your father," he said quietly.

"And?"

"Your kidnapper wants us to do a trade, you for my family, which indicates that he's gotten them away from your father at some point, or something else is going on that we don't yet understand. If the kidnapper is capable of having a career MI6 man doing his bidding, then he could easily have people in your father's organization as well—or vice versa. Your father fired back saying that, if we turn you over to the kidnapper, then my family will never be safe."

She winced. "I'm so sorry," she said. "I don't know how to get either of us out of this mess."

"I know," he said, "and, to make it worse, now we have governments from several countries involved. I don't know that there'll be a happy ending."

She stared at him soberly. "My father is responsible for a lot of deaths now, isn't he?"

"Deaths on American soil, yes," he said quietly.

She stared out the glass window on her door. "Any

chance I could get asylum in the US?"

"Is that what you would like to do?"

"I'd like a new start somewhere," she said.

"And what about your fiancé?"

"Well, as you know, I haven't had news of him for some time. I would hope that he could join me, but I don't even know—"

"Hopefully that will work out for you. So is the US where you would want to be?"

"Even asylum in England would work for me actually."

"But both of them, your father and your kidnapper, could get you a little easier there."

"Maybe," she said, "it depends on how this all plays out and who's left at the end of the day."

He admired her pragmatism in a difficult situation, and, with a note of humor in his voice, he said, "I gather you're not interested in being a captive again."

She shot him a hard look. "Six months was long enough," she said.

"I agree," he said, "but I need to get my family back too."

She sighed at that. "It's just so awful to think that they treat people like chess pieces."

"How much do you have to do with your father's business?"

"I haven't had anything to do with my father at all in a very long time," she said. "I think the only reason he really seemed to care is the fact that I'm his only living relative. And, now that I have a daughter, the line will continue."

"But he has no sons. Does that matter?"

"I don't know," she said. "I've never really felt that from him. The fact is that he doesn't have a son. There is nothing

I can do about that."

"Let me see if I can find out what's happening in terms of what the governments are willing to invest in," he said.

"And find out," she said, "if maybe I could stay in either one of them."

"I will," he said. "We're not far off from British waters right now."

"I do have friends here," she said. "And access to money of my own. I just need to have a safe place to live and where my daughter can grow up without fear."

"But if you have to look over your shoulder forever," he said, "that'll never happen."

"You need to take care of that guy," she whispered. "Both of them."

"I hear you, but that won't be all that easy. I need to know where my family is first."

She nodded slowly. "In my country, I fear they would have just killed them."

"But we're not there," he said, "and it's your country that brought this to ours."

"I'm so sorry about that," she said. "And I'm really sorry for your family."

"I am too," he said, and, with that, he turned and walked out.

CHAPTER 12

WHEN SHELLY WOKE again, Shane walked in her room, pushing a trolley. She looked at it and laughed. "I hope you intend on joining me."

"Absolutely," he said.

She sat up slowly, rubbing her eyes. "Breakfast? Or is it brunch already?"

"It's definitely on the brunch side," he said. He looked exhausted.

"Are you okay?" she asked.

"Yes, I'm fine, but we're still no closer to finding my family."

"And you couldn't roust out anything?"

"Our team was working to follow the traffic cams from her home, but we lost them in the San Diego warehouse district."

"And what about the exchange that this kidnapper guy wants? Wait. The father and the kidnapper both want different deals, right?"

"Exactly. Regardless, the trouble is, even if we get my sister back, there is nothing saying that she or you or Aleah couldn't be targeted again. By the father or the kidnapper."

"So, you need to go on an undercover mission and take them down, right?"

"Right, but it's easier to say than actually accomplish,"

he murmured.

"Got it," she said. "I'm sure you'll do the right thing."

He looked at her, smiled, and said, "Life's easy if you have a Pollyanna attitude about everything."

"After this week, I am very aware that life's not quite so easy as that," she said, "and I also don't want you to get injured or hurt to the extent that I lose you."

He looked up in surprise. "I have no intention of you losing me." He added, "But I also don't want to lose my sister and her family either."

"So what's next?"

"If we can track down where the father took my family in the warehouse district, and then how and where Aleah's kidnapper got them and moved them," he said, "we'll get a team in to confirm they're there and extract them," he said. "But, at the same time, we need to get the boss, Aleah's kidnapper, or it could happen again."

"And Aleah's father?"

"I think he's on his way to England," he said. "He wants his daughter back."

"But," she asked, "does the daughter want to go back?" Shane looked at her, smiling at her response, appreciating again how well she saw the larger picture and got to the point. "She doesn't, does she?"

"I think she's quite done with being a pawn in a man's game," he said.

She nodded. "And yet her father was refusing to do whatever this guy wanted," she said. "So doesn't that make him the good guy?"

"Until you realize that he was quite prepared to kill all those people at your job in order to find somebody who would get his daughter back. Not to mention, taking you and my family to force me to do it."

"So why does he care so much? They clearly don't seem close."

"Well, she's his only living relative for one thing," he said. "And she just had a baby, which continues his line."

"I guess," she said. "Maybe when he realized he was the last of the males of the family, maybe that made a difference finally."

"Well, you'd like to think so," he said, "but I know she wants well out of it."

"I do too," she said. "I definitely do too."

"Well, let's put an end to this mess," he said. "Then I'll help you go wherever you want to go."

She smiled at that. "Why don't you save Prissy and figure out how to get Aleah's father to stop playing games with his daughter and get him away from whatever this problem is with the guy who kidnapped her."

"That is a pretty tall order," he said. And his voice turned even more somber, as he said, "Things like this generally don't have a happy ending."

"Meaning, there'll be some more deaths before it's over?"

As he nodded, she gave him a flat look. "Honestly I'm surprised there hasn't been more already," she said.

"But your coworkers were all innocent people who had nothing to do with any of this," he said. "We can't minimize those lives because we're worried about more deaths."

"Let's get this finished, so at least their lives and their deaths mean something," she said.

"I can get behind that," he said quietly. "I'll have to leave you here, you know?"

"Really?" she said, groaning.

"Really. You've been kidnapped twice," he said. "I can't

have that happen again."

"It was hardly your fault either time," she protested. "And we can't stay on the destroyer as the navy's guests forever either," she said. "I'm not ill, and I know that Aleah wants to get on with her life."

"I'm sure she does. She plans to stay here in England."

"Then let me stay with her," she said. "Just think. The security would be much easier, if you were looking after both of us at the same place." He hesitated, and she pushed her advantage. "We'd be together. I'd help her with the baby. She could get back on her feet and regain some strength," she said. "And we'll both be safe and have a new friend for support, and you'd only have to guard one space."

"I'll see," he said in a noncommittal tone.

"Which means, you'll go away, think about it, and decide I'm right and then come back," she said. "Got it. I'll plan for that." He burst out laughing, shook his head, dropped another kiss on her cheek. Only this time she turned, pulled him down, gave him a real kiss.

He raised his eyebrows at that. "That's a dangerous game."

"Ha!" she said. "I've been living in danger lately."

"You have, indeed," he said. "So, if you want to pick that up where you just stopped, maybe we can wait until it's … until we have a little more time."

"Absolutely," she said, with a smile. "Just maybe we should, … ah, … discuss it?"

"I'm not sure *discussing* is the right thing to do here," he said, studying her with that intense gaze. "Just remember. You opened that door."

She smiled. "I don't regret it either."

"Good to know," he said. "Neither do I." And, with

that, he was gone.

She settled back and smiled at the doorway.

The nurse walked in and said, "Wow, there's a smile."

"It is, indeed," she said. "Change is in the air."

"Good change?"

"I think it must be," Shelly said, "because it feels right."

"Well, that's often a good sign," the nurse said.

Shelly looked at her and asked, "Any chance I can visit the new mom?"

She looked at her in surprise and said, "You know what? Maybe. But let me see how she feels about it."

"Perfect," she said, "you go ahead, and I'll make my way down there."

"I won't have time to get back in the meantime," the nurse said, protesting.

"Oh, I'm not moving very quickly just now, so you'll have plenty of time," she said. The nurse disappeared. And Shelly got to her feet where she put on the slippers and grabbed the little housecoat they had given her, and slowly and steadily made her way down the hallway several doors from her.

When the nurse came out, she smiled. "As it turns out, she would love to meet you."

With a broad smile, Shelly opened the door and stepped inside. "Hi, Aleah," she said, winking at the nurse and stepping forward. "I'm Shelly."

Aleah looked up, smiled, and said, "You are Shane's girl-friend."

"I am, indeed," she said, liking the sound of that. She knew it was a bit presumptuous of her, but, hey, she was nothing if not a person willing to grab the reins and go for it. She took a detour to check on the baby, smiling to see the little angel asleep. "Isn't she perfect? You make pretty babies."

Aleah choked up, tears in her eyes, nodding.

Shelly slowly moved to the other side of Aleah's bed and settled in the visitor's chair, wincing as the movement jarred her forehead.

"Are you okay?" Aleah asked, looking worried.

"I'm fine," she said. "Just, you know, that whole *stitches in the head* thing." She bent her head down, so Aleah could see them.

"Ouch, that's awful. And your poor hair."

At the reference to her hair, she winced. "And I was trying so hard not to even think about the hair," she said, "and now you'll send me running to the mirror to take a look and to see how bad it is."

Aleah burst out laughing.

Smiling, Shelly asked, "So how are you doing, Aleah? You've had a pretty rough time of it."

"I have," she said, "but I'm very happy to say that stage of my life is over."

"Have you had any thoughts about what you want to do now?"

"I was thinking about relocating to the US or England, but, now that I think about it, the UK would be more suited to me," she said. "So I'm hoping I can get that to happen legally."

"I'm guessing that these guys can help arrange something for you," she said, "or at least get you started in the right direction."

"I'm not sure that governments of either country would want anything to do with me because of my father," she said.

"I guess the issue would be whether your father would be

coming to visit."

"No way," she said, "he crossed the line, and we can't go back."

"Which is why the US would probably allow you to come to the States, but they would want to set a trap for him," she said.

Aleah stared at her, with that deep fathomless gaze, then shrugged and nodded. "I was wondering about that myself."

"I'm sorry," she said. "This is a hard way to start motherhood."

"But," she said, with a gentle smile toward the little baby beside her, "at least I got to start it."

"That's very true," Shelly replied. "I hate to ask or seem like I'm prying, but what's the deal with the baby's father?"

"He's off on a military deployment in the US Navy," she said. "I don't even know where he is or if he even knows any of what has happened to me for the last six months. He may think I just ditched him."

"Oh, gosh, that's terrible," Shelly said. "Listen. If you give me his name, maybe we can find a way to contact him."

Aleah looked at her with hope. "Do you think that's possible?"

"I don't know," she said, "but surely somebody's got to tell him that he's a dad at least."

Aleah smiled. "I don't think he knew anything about that either. The whole thing might be just too much of a shock."

"Did he love you?"

"Yes," Aleah said. "We were to get married before he left, but they moved up his departure date, and we couldn't get it arranged fast enough."

"I'm so sorry," she said. "That's terrible."

"It would be fine, I think, if I could actually connect with him and explain."

"Well, give me his name and any information you have about where he might be stationed," she said, "and I'll see what I can find out." With that, Aleah grabbed a napkin off the bedside table, and, using a pen that the nurse had left behind, she quickly wrote down the information. Holding it out, she smiled and said, "Thank you, Shelly. It means a lot that you're even willing to try."

"Hey, when you've got a precious little bundle, like this one," she said, "you do whatever you can."

"You are so right," she said. "Even though she's just hours old, I would do anything for her. It's strange, you know? All those months when I was pregnant, it didn't seem real. I was always terrified that something would happen, and I'd lose her. Especially when I was stuck with those men, and I had literally no one else."

"Did they ever … abuse you or anything like that?"

"No. It was always there, as an implied threat, lording over me, but they never got that far," she said. "I was never really sure what would happen when things inevitably went south. I knew I couldn't count on them to protect me or my baby."

"Well, from what I've heard, it's unlikely that either of them are alive to care at this point," Shelly said.

"I know I should feel bad about that on some level," Aleah said, "but I can't even begin to find that kind of emotion. All I want to focus on is my daughter and some-how creating a new life for the two of us. Hopefully with Renault."

"That sounds like a perfect plan to me," Shelly said. "Life is short as it is, and we've both been through horrific scenarios. We are lucky to have even survived. Whoever would have thought that I'd get kidnapped twice in the same week?"

At that, Aleah's eyes opened wide. "Were you in that telecom building that got blown up by my father?"

"If you mean the one that he had shot up, yes," she said. "I'm the only person from my workgroup who survived."

"Shane got you out of there, didn't he?"

"He did," Shelly said gently. "And I won't take it kindly if anything goes wrong, and he gets hurts too."

"I know," Aleah replied. "I'd feel bad as well. He's gone to so much effort to save me, a complete stranger, and my baby, and I don't want anything to happen to him either."

"Well, let's just keep positive thoughts, and hopefully nothing will." She looked at the sleepy mom and said, "Looks like you are due for a rest again. I'll head back to my room, but it was really nice meeting you and your precious daughter."

SHANE WAS IN his room onboard the naval ship, on the laptop, working side by side with Diesel, when a message from Gavin came up in the chat window.

No more messages from either party.
Decisions?
Your call, Shane.

"Let's take out both of those assholes," he said out loud, then typed a similar message in the chat box.

Agreed, Gavin replied.

We need their locations so we can make a plan.
I'm afraid we'll have to draw them out, Gavin said.

Shane took a long deep breath. **I don't want to use the women as bait.**

They already are.

They don't have to stay that way, Shane argued.

Better answer?

Shane looked at Diesel. "Gavin's asking if we have a better solution than using the women as bait."

Diesel immediately winced.

"I know, right? It goes against everything I believe in," Shane said.

"The thing is, they already are bait, and both men will come after them," he said. "Really, the best thing we can do is set up something to catch both father and kidnapper at the same time."

"Doesn't that make the women bait?"

"I think it's all about the motivation behind it," Diesel said.

"Still sounds like they're bait," Shane said bluntly.

"We'll protect them," Diesel said. "That's already a given. In this case, it means that we'll have to do our utmost to protect them and to set a trap, knowing that neither of these men will ever let it go."

"We could slip the women out and hide them somewhere else."

"We could, but we also know there's a good chance that both of these men have the connections to find out where they are."

"That's true," Shane said. "Shelly's guard from MI6 was a good example of that. I nearly got her killed by protecting her."

"Exactly," Diesel said. "So the question is this. What can we do to minimize the risk to them, keep them secure, and set a trap at the same time?"

"I won't do it if they don't know full well what's happening and the risks they are taking."

"They'll know full well because they already do. These are smart women, and believe me, they are already aware that these guys just won't stop. Trust me. They already know," Diesel said.

Hopping to his feet, Shane said, "I'll go talk to them."

"You do that," Diesel said. "I don't like it either, but I think it's the fastest and most direct way to resolve this thing for good."

"I want to take them both out."

"You won't get any argument out of me for that. We've got one wanted for the murder of eleven innocents that we know of just this week, and the other one held a pregnant woman for six months. And the way it's looking now, they both may have been complicit in taking your family captive."

"That's the other thing," he said. "We need to find my sister."

Just then came a beep, signaling a new message on the chat.

Family possibly located. Gavin went on to mention a block of warehouse buildings.

What did you find? Shane typed.

Finally found them on the cameras. A link was the next thing to populate the chat screen. Pictures of an SUV pulling up in front of a big warehouse. It was hard to identify his brother-in-law for certain, but there was no doubting his sister, who was a tall, slim fiery redhead. She carried one of their kids and had the other by the hand. As Shane watched, they disappeared out of the view of the camera, but this was the best lead they'd gotten.

Address?
Still in San Diego, near a warehouse wharf.

Unaware of the ongoing chat, Diesel continued their conversation. "I wouldn't give Shelly and Aleah too many ideas or specific concerns to think about at the moment," he warned. "They both have some serious healing to do."

Shane nodded, clearly distant now, as he watched the screen for a response, his mind spinning in a totally different direction. "Gavin thinks he's found my family."

Diesel hopped to his feet. "It's about time we got a break," he said. "That's a game changer."

Shane looked at Diesel and said, "We need to move in, rescue them, then set a trap for these assholes."

"Do you think the kidnapper will be where your family is?"

"I doubt it," he said, "but which one has his goons on site? We're not even positive who has them now and how this is all related. The one guy is still after something from Aleah's father. The more leverage he has against the father, the less he'll care about my family. I already did my job and got Aleah away."

"Sure, but you did too good of a job. The kidnapper's keeping the pressure on you no matter what, so you keep Aleah from her father. That's got to be why he tried to grab Shelly."

"I know," he said. "The trouble is, with guys like this, they could have infiltrated each other's organizations too. So, no matter what we think is going on, we'll have to really be on our toes."

"Both men are a danger to Shelly and Aleah, no doubt."

"Poor Aleah. This will be bad for her, no matter how it goes."

"I hear you there," Diesel said slowly. "We'll only get one shot. I wonder if we can set up a handoff with a decoy."

"As long as we've got my family, yes," he said, "but it all has to happen with precision timing."

Diesel gave a lopsided grin. "Good thing that is our specialty."

Shane groaned. "It'd be nice to have the tiniest bit of leeway for once."

"But that's not the way it ever works," Diesel said. "We just have to deal with it, and we have to deal with it now. You know the consequences if we don't."

Unfortunately he did. All too well.

CHAPTER 13

S HELLY WAS QUICKLY ushered into a small room on the second floor of the little house, where she turned and stared at Shane. "Are you sure this is the best answer?"

"It's a combination of your idea and mine," he said quietly.

"It's not that we're bait," she said, reaching up to pat his cheek. "Just quit looking at it that way."

He nodded. "I hear you. I do. But I really don't like it. I'd rather have you safely tucked away, somewhere far away from here."

"But you have to admit that the two of us together will be a very tantalizing prospect."

"No doubt. We suspect that still another mole is somewhere in the kidnapper's organization or the father's organization, probably within MI6 again, considering the first one was there," he said. "So, all of our attempts to keep things secret weren't enough back then anyway."

"So the plan is to keep us together, to stay with us, and to presume that somebody will make a move."

"I'd move on that," he said. "We've decided that the best way to predict their actions to get at you two is to go with the strategy we would utilize ourselves."

"That's why you were hired in the first place," she said, "because you could get the job done."

"Yeah, but I'm not alone," he said, "and now that Aleah is out of that kidnap situation, and we're hardly under heavy guard here," he said, "somebody is likely to try again."

"I get that," she said, turning to stare at her small bedroom. "Have you got her safely ensconced on the other side?"

"Yes," he said. "You two can share this upper apartment, with the kitchen, a little closet, bathroom, all the necessities, so you don't need to be going anywhere else. Stay inside. Please stay on this floor."

"And for the baby?" she asked.

"Yes, things are set up for the baby too." He reached over and peered at her stitches.

"I'm fine," she said crossly.

"Well, you will be fine," he snapped. "You're just not quite there yet."

She glared at him, and he glared right back. She burst out laughing, then reached up and gave him a gentle kiss. "Hurry back."

"We'll have to deal with this when I do," he said, his gaze narrowing.

"Nothing to deal with," she said.

"Sounds like you've changed the game."

"I have?" she asked in surprise. She opened her eyes wide and stared at him and said, "I think … this was always there, just maybe on the sidelines somewhere."

"Maybe," he said, "but it's been like an unwritten rule that we had between us not to get involved."

"Yeah, absolutely," she said. "Do you want to change that?" He opened his mouth and closed it. She nodded. "Yeah, I jumped in and put that question to you before you could put it to me."

"Not fair," he muttered.

She burst out laughing again, walked over, and gave him a big hug. "It's tough times right now," she murmured.

"It would be a whole lot less tough if you weren't always distracting me."

"Distracting? I don't think that's the real reason," she said.

"You're dancing around the issue," he said calmly.

"Maybe." She nodded. "But it's hardly the time or place."

"True, but it is distracting me," he said, "and I don't like it." His voice turned hard, and he glared at her.

She gave him a cheeky smile and said, "Still like to have all the answers locked down first, don't you?"

"Yes, and so do you," he said with a nod. "So where are we going?"

"Where would you like to go?" she asked.

"No answering a question with a question," he said. "That's called deflection."

She smiled and said, "Fine. I would like to see where a romantic relationship between the two of us could go," she admitted. "We've never come to this point before. We always had other people in our lives."

"I never looked at you that way before," he said cautiously.

"Didn't you?" She frowned. "So maybe you don't feel anything then." She took several steps back. "Maybe this is just on my side. In which case I'll have to sit down and take another look at that."

"I didn't say that," he said, his tone grumbling.

She looked at him. "No, you didn't, but you're not saying anything in the other direction either." She took another

171

step back, shoved her hands in her pockets, and said, "Go on and save the world now. We'll be fine here."

She picked up her bag and placed it on the bed, ready to unpack her few things. Inside, she was shaking. She had been so damn sure that he felt for her what she felt for him that it had never occurred to her that he was completely flummoxed by it all. Or that he wasn't in the same boat. She'd never felt lonelier in her life, as if everything in her world had just come crashing down. Yet she had no idea why. She'd never thought of him as a lover until this mess.

But he'd been the first one she would have depended on and the first person she'd call if she were in trouble. Even now, the thought of going back to California felt right because he was there. How much of what she wanted was because he would be there? She slowly sat down on the edge of the bed. When she heard his voice again, she looked at him, startled, because somehow she thought he had left. "What?" she asked.

"I said, *I care*," he grumbled.

"I'm sorry. Of course you care," she said. "We're friends. We've been good friends for a really long time."

"Exactly," he said. "It's not a good idea to change that."

"That's just old talk in your head," she said, with a wave of her hand. "The bottom line is, if you don't feel anything, then that's just the way it is," she said. "It doesn't matter what good old friends we are or whether this is what I want or not. It has to be mutual. And, if that's not the case, then nothing is here. So we'll just go back to being friends. It's not like we ever changed that anyway."

She got up and resumed putting away her things. As she went back to the bed for the third trip, studiously ignoring the big stalwart presence in the small room, she was snatched into his arms and held against him. She looked up at him in surprise. "What brought this on?"

"You," he said in despair.

"It's okay," she said. "We're still friends. That'll never change."

"Yes, it will."

She wrapped her arms around him. "It's okay, you know?"

He shook his head, as if unable to speak, then his arms crushed her even tighter against him. She settled in, not sure what was going on, but willing to see where this was going—although she felt the hot tears inside, the tears of loss that he didn't feel what she did.

Finally he let out a deep breath. "I have to leave," he said.

"I know you do," she said, immediately withdrawing.

He shook his head. "No," he said, "I can't leave it like this."

"But you have to go. We don't have time to talk out the whole thing."

"I know," he said. "So this will have to do for now." He gently tilted up her chin, and he crushed her mouth with his, sending shards of passion and heat spiraling through her and shooting down to her toes. By the time he lifted his head, he looked at her with satisfaction. She could barely even keep her eyes open to see him. "Much better," he said, and then he let her go.

She stumbled backward. "What the hell was that all about?" she cried out, reaching out a hand to stabilize herself in a world suddenly awry.

"I couldn't say the right words," he said, "so it felt like action was better."

She stared at him mutely, still dumbfounded. "I see. Do you want to explain that?"

"I think you can figure it out from here. I'll see you when I get back." And, with that, he whistled and headed out the door.

AS HE WALKED away, Shane heard Shelly throwing things at the door, and he laughed out loud. Diesel looked at him, heard the items banging against the wall, the door, the floor, and asked, "What's that all about?"

"We just have to clarify a few things," he said with a big grin.

"Ah, so you'll finally take my advice, will you?" Diesel said, beaming.

"I think I am," he said. "I couldn't find the right words back there just now, but I think I found the right actions."

"Are you sure about that?"

Just then the door opened, and Shelly screamed down the hallway, "Stop scrambling my brain!" Then she slammed it shut again.

Diesel howled. "A perfect match, just like I said."

"Well, better than I thought anyway," Shane said. "I don't know how, but I didn't see it at all."

"Well, it may not have been there before either," Diesel said. "Maybe you both had to get to the same time and place."

"Well, we're there now," he said. "Wow."

"You sure you're ready to head out and do some work now?"

"Yep, we need to make sure this place is safe, or as safe as we can make it."

"And MI6 showed up?"

"Yep, three men."

"And Gavin?"

"He says that two of the MI6 men he trusts. He doesn't know the third one," Shane said.

"Which means we'll automatically look at him as a weak link."

"But no guarantee that he is."

"No, of course not," he said.

"And just thinking about it will put us in the wrong spot."

"Told ya," he said, grinning at his buddy who found love.

"I guess," Shane said. And, as they walked back outside, he turned and looked around. "Can't even see anybody, so that's good."

"You want to just stand guard?"

"I feel like that would be way too obvious."

"Well, it would also give you something to think about other than your family," Diesel said. "And Shelly."

"I would much rather be rescuing my sister right now," he said with a growl.

"Can't afford to be thinking about that. Come on," Diesel said.

"I know, but only because they're still in the US and I'm here in England." They stepped off to the side into the brush, as Shane turned to look around at the small house, settled in a little bit of the countryside, a good twenty miles out of London. With little houses on either side but set on large properties, so they weren't butted up against each other.

"We don't know for sure that anybody knows about this location, right?" Diesel asked.

"No," he said, "and that'll be one of the issues, so we can't slack off."

"But waiting will be hard. We have to do it all at the same time." Just then his phone buzzed. Shane pulled it out to see a text message from Gavin.

Op in progress.

He winced and put it away. "Well, that's not helpful," he muttered. "The op to rescue my sister is in progress, and now I just have to sit here and wait."

As he stood in the shadows, a bullet soared over his head, nearly parting his hair. He swore and dropped to the ground, then turned to see Diesel on the ground beside him. They looked at each other; then they split up, going in opposite directions. Shane wasn't sure what the hell was happening, but, as far as timing went, this one didn't really give them a chance to adjust. He quickly sent a message to Shelly that they were under attack and to stay inside and away from windows. Then he turned off his phone and shoved it in his pocket and headed toward the shooter.

Three other men—MI6—should be out here some-where, supporting their effort to protect the women, but, as Shane raced forward, his foot caught on something, and he hit the ground hard facedown in the shrubs. Pulling himself back up, he turned to see what he had tripped over to find one of the MI6 men dead—dressed in black ops gear, his own weapon still beside him.

Swearing, Shane grabbed the weapons and quickly melt-ed into the shadows. He had no idea how many enemy operatives were here, probably more than they expected. Could be a large group. When a voice called out, he strained to hear it. But then he heard his name.

"Shane, get your ass out in the open. You've got my daughter," he said. "I want her now."

"That may be," he called back, "but you've got my family, or do you?"

"I said I wanted a peaceful exchange."

"Maybe so, but you haven't even taken out the asshole who did this to your daughter."

"Well, he's here too, as it turns out," he said. "We're on a peaceful mission together to make sure we get her back."

"And how is that possible?" Shane cried out.

"The asshole who kidnapped her is the father of her child."

What the hell? he thought to himself, in shock. That's not at all what he had understood from Aleah. When there was no more word, he tried to wrap his mind around that and then shook his head. He didn't believe it. "That's bullshit," he shouted.

The man laughed. "Well, it was worth a try."

"Where's the guy who kidnapped her in the first place?" he said.

"Dead," he snapped.

And there was such a wealth of satisfaction in his voice that Shane tended to believe him, yet he knew he couldn't really trust anything this guy said. Maybe the guy who pulled off the kidnapping was dead, but Shane didn't think the perpetrator behind the kidnapping was dead. "Well, I'll need proof of that," he said.

"Well, you won't get it," he said. "I want my daughter."

"I want my family."

"Well, how about I leave your little girly here alive?" he said. "I could have killed her back in New York, you know?

But I opted to leave you that one."

"I want my family, and I want you to leave them and Shelly alone," he snapped, sidling closer, until he noted where the voice was coming from. And damn if it wasn't from the house beside him. He shook his head. "Did you kill the occupants of that house?"

"Roadkill," he said.

"What if your daughter doesn't want to go with you?"

"Too damn bad," he said. "I've gone through too much to leave her in your care now."

None of this made any sense. "Are you sure she's even your daughter?" Shane asked. "I don't know what the hell's going on here, but, considering how very little contact you've had with her over the years, this doesn't make sense."

Just then Aleah's voice called from inside the house, "Yes, it does make sense now, Shane. My new baby daughter is the heir to a decent fortune," she murmured. "The father of my child, his lineage, combined with my own, that's what my father wants to get his hands on."

"Aleah," her father said, "get out of that house now. Come on. We have to go home."

"I'm not going anywhere with you," she said. "I'm staying in England, where Interpol is looking for you, so you can't very well stay here, much less return."

Shane heard silence, then grumbling.

"No," he said, "you're coming back where you belong."

"Only to get kidnapped again by somebody else in your world? No," she snapped. "I won't."

"I'm not giving you an option," he said.

"I'm not a child anymore, Father. I can live wherever I please."

As their discussion went back and forth, Shane watched

in the shadows, as Diesel shifted his position, and Shane knew things would blow up here very fast.

"You can't have her," Shelly called out. There was a moment of silence and then an ugly response.

"You have no say in the matter, and you just earned yourself a bullet between the eyes."

At that, Shane shifted and looked again to see Diesel coming up on the side of the neighbor's house.

"That won't happen," Shelly yelled, "but you'll get yours. You killed eleven of my coworkers, just to test Shane," she said. "Well, he saved your daughter, and here you are, still being an asshole."

"There are always assholes in the world," the father replied. "You just have to make sure you're the bigger one."

"But you weren't," she said, "because somebody yanked your chain and stole your daughter."

"Well, he's dead," he snapped. "And so are you."

Immediately bullets were fired at the front of the house. As Shane went to step forward, a gun came up against his neck. He froze, dropped to the ground, then kicked and fired. Taken by surprise, his assailant went down without a struggle. At that, Shane noted complete silence surrounded him. Moving quietly through the brush, he headed toward the last sighting of Aleah's father.

Just then came another shout.

"Well, you got one," the father said. "But half a dozen more are out there after you."

At that, Shane froze, then thought about it, and shook his head. He continued to move silently through the trees. At one point, he was almost back up to the road. He stepped in behind a particularly nice wide bush and grabbed the lowest branch of the tree beside him and crawled up. When he was up a good ten feet high, he studied the layout. The front of the house had been riddled with bullets. Lights were on in several neighboring houses, and dogs were barking everywhere.

As far as the father though, he stood in the front of the neighboring house, completely unconcerned about getting shot. Which meant that he either did have a number of men in the woods around here, or he was completely encased in something that would save him. It was too dark to see. He did have something over his face. Even taking a bullet to a bulletproof vest was a hell of a blow though. It could cause bruising and soreness for days.

Just then, as Shane watched, the man stepped back and called out to his daughter again.

"Aleah, come out. I don't want to have to come in there and get you."

"I'm not coming out," she said, in a world-weary voice. "I'll marry Renault, and we'll move to London."

"That won't happen," he said. "You're my only blood, and you have my only grandchild," he said. "You need to come home."

"There's no home for me with you, not like this," she said. "And now that you've senselessly killed so many people, you know Interpol will seek you out for the Americans."

"I did it to save you," he cried out.

"Yes," she said, "you did, but the end result is I can't go anywhere now without knowing that's what you've done. You didn't have to kill those people."

"I did," he said. "There was no other way to make sure they knew I was serious." There was silence at that.

Until, of course, Shelly yelled out, "You didn't have to kill the people in my office. They were completely innocent.

They didn't deserve that."

"None of us deserve anything," the father snapped. "I didn't deserve to have my whole life ripped out from under me when my daughter was kidnapped six months ago."

"I'm surprised that you care," Shelly snapped.

Shane winced, wishing she'd stay quiet, but she was as feisty in captivity as she was at any other point in time.

"I care," he said. "Aleah is my cherished daughter."

"Father, as you well know, we haven't had anything to do with each other in a very long time," Aleah cried out. "I don't understand what's suddenly changed."

Just then a new voice entered the fray. "What's changed is that you are owed to me," the stranger said.

There was a shocked silence, before Aleah called out, "*Owed to you?* What are you talking about?"

"Yes," he said. "You were given to me many, many years ago, when you were just a child. We have a contract, and your father was paid a handsome dowry. When he refused to hand you over, I took you myself," he said. "But imagine how I felt to find out that you were not pure, and, worse than that, you were carrying another man's child."

"Well, since I didn't know anything about this arrangement," she said, "I can hardly be judged for having found somebody I love." In the silence, Aleah's voice cried out again. "Is it true, Father? Did you sell your *cherished daughter* to this man?"

There was still only silence.

"See? He can't answer you to deny my claim. Not only did he receive money but he also received backing. Political backing, financial backing. He cannot step away from this," he said.

"But you don't even want me anymore," she said, her

voice angry.

"I don't want some crying brat, but I will take you," he said. "But you are certainly not what I expected, so you won't be my only wife. But together we will have children."

Jesus, Shane thought to himself. *What the hell is this?* But, of course, in these other cultures, particularly anywhere in the Middle East, the rules of family and marriage were very different, and difficult for women, who were little more than possessions.

As Shane listened, Shelly piped up, "She's already made a choice, and you weren't it. She loves the father of her child, and she wants to spend her life with him. You made a pact with the devil, so deal with the devil yourself."

At that, the stranger gave a snort. "That's not a bad idea," he said. "If he can't return the money and pay me back for all the other benefits he enjoyed, he might as well be dead."

At that, Shane slipped down the tree and raced forward, until he came up on the other side of the house.

Aleah's father called out, "We have an agreement, a pact. He'll say whatever he can to get you out, but he won't shoot me any more than I'll shoot him."

"Are you so sure about that?" The stranger's silky voice permeated through the darkness once again.

"Yes," the father said, "because I am privy to an awful lot of secrets that you don't want revealed."

"Just like the information I have on you," the stranger said.

"Therefore, we protect each other as planned."

"Or I just shoot you, and any secrets you hold stay hidden," the man said.

"Aw, but then you have to trust that I haven't implemented a plan to send the secrets out to the world upon my death," he said calmly.

Such a sense of arrogant assurance filled Aleah's father's voice that Shane wasn't sure who or what to believe. "They're both nuts," he whispered to himself. Nobody was around him in the darkness. Pulling out his muted phone, he sent Diesel a message. **Anyone around you? I have one down.**

One down here, Diesel replied.

Any idea how many more?

No. But there has to be several.

Just as Shane was thinking about returning to the woods again, a shot rang out close to the house. He swore silently because he hadn't left any weapons with Shelly and Aleah. And that he couldn't stand. He studied the countryside, slipped back toward the trees, and, just as a verbal exchange broke out again between the two men, still fighting for control, Shane slipped up behind the house.

Moving silently and below window height, he slipped in through a downstairs window. Once inside, he stood, gun at the ready, and didn't even see the blow that came out of nowhere. He dropped to his knees, as the pain made his skull feel like a ratchet had been used on him. But he bounced back up as fast as he could and took on his attacker. The fight was hard, furious, and completely in darkness.

He was amazed when he landed the few punches he did, but, once he had the man in a headlock, he didn't stop until his adversary sagged in his arms, completely unconscious. Pulling his phone back out, he checked his victim with the Flashlight mode and sent a snapshot to Diesel. Stripping his captive of his weapons, Shane tied up the man and left him under the window.

Then he sent a text back to Diesel. **Headed for the stairs.** Keeping low, he quickly made his way through to Aleah's room. It was empty. He headed to Shelly's room and found the two women huddled on the floor of the closet. They both started when they saw him. He held a finger to his lips. Shelly scrambled toward him. He gave her a quick hug and whispered, "Go back and sit with her again."

He noted that the baby was tucked up in blankets and that they were half in the closet. He motioned for them to get farther back into the closet, and he partially closed the door and then pulled the mattress off the bed and put it up in front of them. With any luck, errant bullets would get lodged or at least deflected before going any farther. With that, he did a quick sweep of the house but found nobody else inside. He stayed low when he heard the men outside arguing again. He left the bedroom and headed for the front door.

CHAPTER 14

S HELLY WANTED TO race behind Shane, and, even as she shifted, Aleah grabbed her arm and whispered, "Stay here."

Shelly looked at Aleah, the baby tucked up close to her, and the fear in Aleah's eyes. Shelly settled back and nodded. "He's good," she said. "We can trust him."

"I don't know how to trust," Aleah said quietly, "when they lie, and they cheat, and they steal."

"Not all of them," she said.

Aleah nodded. "All of them."

"Even the father of your child?"

"Well, no," she said, stopping, looking confused. "But he's young."

"He doesn't have to turn out that way either," Shelly said. "Not all men are like your father or this asshole out here who bought you."

"It's often the way in my country," she said. "This arrangement they spoke of would help to explain why my father rose so high up, becoming what he is."

"He had a lot of backing, I presume."

"Yes. It's all making sense to me now. My family has royal heritage," she said, "but no money to speak of, no real standing. This man had money and power but lacked the lineage. That is what he was buying me for, ... access to the lineage. In the meantime, over all these years, my father used the dowry to become an even more terrible man than he was."

"And now you've messed it all up by having a child," she said.

"I didn't even know about this arrangement of theirs," she said, "and I wouldn't have cared."

"No, I get that," Shelly said, "because I'd be the same way. But the bottom line is that he won't treat you very nicely because you've already had another man's child."

Aleah's eyes widened. "No," she said, "he won't. He isn't a nice man anyway, and this has just made it all worse."

"But would he still marry you and force having his children on you if he gets a chance?"

"Absolutely. Then he'll take his children from me, and I'll be an accidental death somewhere in the not-too-distant future."

"And I presume your father won't care either way?"

"No. He's got his money out of me already."

"In that case, why do you think he's trying to rescue you now?"

"I don't know that he is. It may be a matter of making sure I comply," she said quietly. "When he found out I was pregnant, he was absolutely livid."

"The baby's father, do you think his life is in danger?"

At that, Aleah gasped, stared at her, and asked, "Do you think so?"

"Well, he's the one who led you astray, in their minds, so to speak. Sorry to use such an old-fashioned phrase."

"I think my father just wanted me as collateral again, to hold over the man he sold me to and to exploit the lineage of my baby's father."

"Could your father be trying to stop that man in any way?"

"Well, they could renegotiate a deal maybe? One that would get my father off the hook because, above all else, my arranged husband wants the lineage. He doesn't so much care beyond that."

"So even though you've given birth to another man's child, he'll forgive that?"

"Well, he says he will. But, once I'm married to him," she said, "there's absolutely nothing anyone can do to stop his abuse."

"Maybe he won't though."

"He already has," she said. "He was livid when he found out I was pregnant and hit me several times. At the time, I thought he wanted to sell me into the sex trade. So I worried that he would kill my child, to sell me sooner. But I made it very clear that, if he killed my baby, I would kill myself. Little did I know he wanted me himself."

"Either way, he would never get what he wanted."

She shook her head.

"I'm so sorry, Aleah. These past six months must have been even more horrible with all that hanging over your head. So, what's the deal with your father?"

"That I still don't quite understand, except maybe he feels that, as long as he saves me, he can take my baby, his grandchild, and maybe use that to his own gain. I don't know." She shrugged. "And it doesn't matter. As much as anything I think he knows that I need to become this man's wife to get himself off the hook."

"And yet," she said, "he didn't wait until you were married to the man to get you out. That says something good, right?"

"There would be no point then because, if we were married, I would be deemed his property. No," she said, "in our culture, it would shame him to marry a pregnant woman. He wants our lineage and the people's respect. So he had to wait for the birth of the baby. Maybe that is what my father and he are arguing about? For he had me and my baby in a real sense, whether I had given birth yet or not. He was probably auctioning off my child to my father. Oh my. I didn't think it could be worse than I already thought." Aleah stared in horror, as Shelly patted her hand.

"My father must have realized, without even telling me about this arrangement, that I would never marry any man over some archaic dowry deal. He's probably been stalling for years, but then my intended finally put his foot down and kidnapped me, hoping to marry, not knowing of my pregnancy. That's why he held me for so long. Meanwhile, my father's desperate to find some angle, some deal that he can make out of it that saves him and grants him possession of his grandchild."

"I don't think anybody'll get saved out of this mess," she said. "Your father may have planned to save you for whatever reason, but I don't know if it was for your best interests or his."

"His," she said immediately. "It's always about his."

"In which case, either he'll save himself or get something out of this deal."

"That's right. He's bled the guy as much as he can, and that's blowing up in his face. So now he's discovered that my baby has wealth via her father's lineage, so he'll probably get me back, so I can have more children with Renault."

"Wow, that all sounds worse and worse," she muttered, "and I don't see either of the two men outside stopping. We need to get rid of these guys."

She gave a broken laugh. "And how am I to do that?"

Shelly asked, "What's your father's name?"

"Aziz," she said.

Shelly lifted her voice. "Aziz, your daughter doesn't want to go back. She doesn't want to marry the guy you sold her to, and she doesn't want to live with you." There was silence.

"What she wants does not matter," he said, his voice coming closer.

"How is it you feel you can ruin your daughter's life? How old was your little girl when you sold her future to this evil man?"

"She's my daughter. She's my property. I will make the decisions."

"You already made a decision. Then this man kidnapped her."

"Yes, she is to marry him."

"Then why would you even try to get her back again? Why go through that ridiculous testing process to make sure Shane was good enough to rescue your daughter, if her kidnapper is the man who's to marry her anyway?"

"Because they must be married," he said. "That is a given. However, at this point I also need to obtain some assurances on my life, on my grandchild. Because Aleah has defied me and defiled herself by getting pregnant, the deal will be different."

"Ah, now she's secondhand goods, is that it?"

"Yes, as you Americans would say it. Exactly."

"Well, that won't work out for me," Shelly said. She lifted her head and peered around the corner of the closet door and mattress. "I don't know where the guys are," she whispered to Aleah, "but they need to grab Aziz fast. I can only distract him for so long."

Aleah looked at her in surprise. "You say these things to upset my father, and what good will that do?"

"Maybe he'll give away his position. Maybe somebody will take out one of them. I don't know," she said. "What I do know is that, if he comes in here, I'm dead. He'll try to send you off to get married, but he'll shoot me on the spot."

At that, Aleah nodded slowly. "Yes, that's true. My father will kill you."

"So, at this point, anything I do," Shelly said in a hard voice, "is to help my situation and yours."

"You are confusing," she said, "and I don't see how antagonizing him can help."

Well, Shelly didn't really either. But it made her feel good, so, if antagonizing this asshole was the last thing she did in this world, well, so be it. She sent out a quiet prayer to Shane. *I hope you know what you're doing because I need to get out of here.* But then this wasn't the tightest or the worst situation she'd been in before, and Shane had been the one who had rescued her then as well. Besides, they had a whole new life ahead of them. She wouldn't condone or support anything that took what could be a very bright future away from her. She looked around, then looked back at Aleah. "Wait here."

She quietly slipped out of the closet and around the mattress to the door that was open and crawled out into the hallway. There she watched as Shane, standing up against the common room wall, slowly cut a circle of glass out of the window, then raised his weapon. She watched in amazement as he took a slow deep breath and pulled the trigger.

⚓

THE MAN'S HEAD exploded.

Shane quickly withdrew his rifle as gunfire rapidly returned in his direction. A second shot rang out, and then there was nothing but silence. He twisted to see Shelly, who he'd heard creeping along the carpet. He held a finger to his lips. She nodded. He knew she was struggling to stay put and out of the way, but he had hoped she would have lasted a little bit longer. But then that was expecting too much.

At the sound of a weird bird call, her eyes widened, but Shane just shook his head and answered it. Immediately there was another call. She crawled toward Shane, and, when she got to where he stood, he gave her a hand up, putting her back against the wall.

She whispered, "What was that?"

"Diesel."

"Is he giving you an all clear?"

"Well, we're hoping so. We'll have to figure out how many men are left."

"Who did you shoot?"

He took a look at her and said, "Her father."

She winced and nodded. "Good," she said. "That other asshole needs to die too."

"It seems like the two men have been after each other for a long time. Half-friends, half-enemies," he said. "The research we found on them was very convoluted. They have been a strange combination of business partners, enemies, and friends for a very long time. But now, with the arranged marriage disclosure, it makes more sense."

"Well, you shot and killed Aziz. Now what will the intended groom do?"

"He plans to kill us all," Shane said. At Shelly's worried look, he said, "Except possibly Aleah. And I won't be so easy to kill."

"And so he'll kill me?" Shelly asked.

Shane closed his eyes and whispered, "You're right. We still have one asshole."

"Now," the gunman yelled, "I want the three of you to get out of that house before I blow it up."

"What about Aleah?" Shane asked aloud, then whispered to Shelly, "Take Aleah and the baby, leave through the back door, and run, fast."

The gunman yelled once more, "What about her? If I can't have her, I'll find another one," he said. "She's secondhand goods anyway. Now I'll let you count to ten, and, by then, you better have that front door open and be coming out," he said, "or I'll set off the bomb."

Diesel called out, "He's holding a detonator in his hand."

"Absolutely I am," he said.

"Who was the mole who told you where we were?"

"An MI6 informant," he said. "Even though he was discovered and suspended from duty, they hadn't removed his access from everything, so we were still tapped in to his plans. But he's dead now too. I couldn't afford to leave him as a loose end. Once I'm gone from here, I'm gone," he said.

The dead MI6 agent in the grass here. "And you'll kill Aleah too then?"

"If she doesn't come out, she dies," he said. "I've invested enough time and money in this."

Aleah. Immediately Shane dashed down the stairs toward the back door. He met up with the women, pushed them as fast as he could to the kitchen door, and, as soon as he opened it, he ordered them to head straight into the brush and to run as fast as they could.

"There could be shooters out there," he said, "so dodge, move to the side, do whatever you have to, but get into hiding and stay there." He took the baby from Aleah and said, "Let me carry this one." And, with that, he raced behind them. They barely made it past the far corner, when the house exploded with a loud *boom.*

CHAPTER 15

THEY SETTLED INTO the brush away from the house. Shelly stared at Shane in shock. Aleah was huddled up against her, still not recovered from giving birth, still in pain and still sore, but clutching her baby tightly against her. "Jesus," Shelly said, "these people need to stop."

"They will," Shane said, "after one last hurrah. You stay here and don't move. "Keep the baby quiet and don't make a sound." Then he looked at Shelly and added, "I mean it this time." Then he turned and raced away.

"He knows you well, doesn't he?" Aleah muttered.

"Apparently." She sat down beside her and said, "We need to make sure that they can't find us."

"The house fire will make it hard for us to hide," Aleah said. "I'll bet our faces show up easily."

"Good point." Shelly carefully disguised the baby with her blanket and their faces with a shield of branches. "There. That's better. Now we stay here and try not to move," she whispered. They heard gunfire and sounds of fighting. It all made her heart run cold. Aleah reached over, grabbed her hand, and hung on. Shelly squeezed her hand back and whispered, "Hold tight. This will be over soon."

"It will be, but who will be the winner?" Aleah whispered.

"Shane," Shelly said, "it will be Shane."

And, at that, a man almost beside them said, "You're right. It's over. But Shane winning? Not happening."

She gasped and tightened her grip on Aleah. The branches were pulled back, and she stared up at a Middle Eastern man with a rifle pointed at them. Shelly looked up at him and said, "Hi, apparently you're the one who wanted this woman for your wife."

He snorted, then looked at Aleah and back to Shelly in disgust. "Women. Too much trouble."

As he raised the rifle in their direction, Shelly immediately bolted forward, hitting the barrel of the rifle up high into the air, as it fired harmlessly again and again. The gunman smacked her hard across the side of her face, and she cried out from the blow. She fell haphazardly to her knees and then turned to see him holding the rifle on Aleah. She was terrified, as she held the tiny baby close against her chest. When the baby cried, Shelly reached out, put her hand against him. "Don't. They don't deserve this."

He glared at her. "You all die now."

She shook her head, seeing Shane coming up on the side, his weapon drawn. She looked at him and recognized he was discreetly motioning, telling her to step away.

Smiling up at the gunman, she said, "You're wrong. But don't believe me." With that, she threw herself down in front of Aleah, and immediately a shot rang out. She turned to see the gunman standing there, a shocked look on his face, as he stared down at the women, then slowly sank to his knees and fell over sideways. Aleah burst into tears, and Shelly could only hold her tight, the baby crying in her arms.

Immediately Shane raced toward them. "Are you two all right?"

"The three of us are fine," Shelly said, looking up at

him. "Is it over?"

He nodded. "I think so. But I need to do another round to make sure there are no other gunmen."

She motioned at him. "Go then," she said. "Make sure they're all dead. I'll keep his weapon here."

He nodded and asked, "Do you know how to use it?"

"No," she said, "but believe me. I'll figure it out in a pinch."

He gave a hard laugh and said, "That's my girl." And he took off.

Shelly sat here, with Aleah trembling at her side, the baby tucked up against her mother, now happily nursing.

"Just hold that baby," she said. "This will get better now."

"How do I ever thank you?" she said. "To be forced to be with him would have been—"

"Not fun," she said. "But he's gone now." Shelly stared at the man and shook her head. "You know what? I've seen more deaths in the last few days …"

"I'm sorry," Aleah said. "You didn't deserve to be brought into this mess. This is my family's fault," she said, shaking her head.

"*Was* your family," Shelly reminded her. "Listen, Aleah. I've waited to tell you, but, well, your father's dead too."

"Good," she said passionately. "I've never had anything much to do with him. He treated my mother so terribly. Then to find out that he actually sold me, just a child, and promised me to a man like that. All these years he's acted like such a mighty and powerful man, but it was all a lie, and he's been living off the fruits of that betrayal. No wonder my mother died so young."

"I'm sorry," she said. "Obviously a lot of changes are

about to happen in your world."

"After what I've been through already," she said, "bring it on."

Shelly laughed. "That's the spirit," she said. "We'll need to get you some legal status here in England and make sure you have a place to live and that the baby will be fine," she said. "But, for right now, we just need to sit here, until it's all clear."

Sure enough, both Diesel and Shane returned within minutes. They helped Aleah to her feet, and, realizing she had no shoes on, Diesel quickly picked up her and her baby and carried them around the burning house.

Hearing sirens approach in the distance, Shelly looked at Shane. "Do we need to get out of here before they arrive?"

"Absolutely," he said. "Mavericks don't stick around for explanations if they can avoid it." Quickly they climbed into a black vehicle and drove off, traveling several blocks, before seeing the emergency vehicles. Shane looked at Shelly. "Are you okay?"

"I'm fine," she said, "just damn glad it's over with."

"Me too."

Shelly glanced at Diesel. "Did you get hurt?"

"Nope," he said, "that was a clean run for me."

"I don't know how you guys can do this all the time," Shelly said, yawning. "I'm exhausted."

"Well, we'll find a hotel," Shane said. He looked at Aleah. "Are you doing okay?"

Aleah nodded. "Now I am," she said. "Now I know I'll be fine."

"Maybe we'll find a surprise at the hotel."

Aleah just looked at him and said, "Honestly I don't need any more surprises. I just want a calm, quiet place to raise my daughter."

"Yep," Shane said but didn't elaborate.

"I wouldn't mind a surprise," Shelly said. "Like maybe a hot dog or something. I'm starving." By the time they got to the hotel, a good forty minutes away, Shelly was tired but keyed up. There had been far too much adrenaline, too much pain, too much shock, too much everything, and she was just wired. They got out slowly, and she felt her body groan and complain with the movement. When she stood, Shane looked at her, smiled, and said, "You look like you could use a hot shower."

"How about a hot dog?" she asked.

"Right," he said, "we'll see about that, after we get you ladies settled." They got Shelly and Aleah up to their rooms, which had adjoining doors. He spoke to the tired young mother and said, "We already ordered some basic supplies for the baby. We'll bring them up when they get here."

She nodded her thanks. "I just need to get some sleep."

"Yeah, maybe so," he said. At the knock on the door, he walked over, turned, looked at her, and said, "You might also need this too."

He opened the door to reveal a young man of maybe twenty-six or twenty-seven, standing in the doorway, looking at Shane in surprise and frowning.

He said, "Sorry, I was told to come here." Then he turned and took one look at Aleah on the bed, holding the baby. His facial expressions went through myriad emotions but finally settled on pure unadulterated love, as he raced across the room to gather the two of them in his arms. Aleah immediately broke into tears and buried her face against the side of his neck, sobbing with joy and relief.

Shelly walked over and wrapped her arms around Shane

and said, "That was a good thing you did."

"Well, we do have pull in some high places," he said. "They'll have to work things out on their own going forward, but this is what we could do for them now."

"That's a lot," she murmured.

He smiled, nodded, and said, "Now let's see what we can do to get you taken care of." They quickly closed the connecting door, and there was her bedroom. She looked around and said, "I don't even know what happened to my overnight bag."

"It's probably still in the house on fire," he said cheerfully.

She groaned. "So far I haven't had a whole lot of luck keeping things safe around you."

"Well, if you would listen to my instructions every once in a while," he said.

"That won't happen," she replied, then walked into the bathroom. Grinning at the size of the bathtub, she said, "I'll have a bath. I feel smoky, dirty, and incredibly tired."

"What about food?" he asked.

"Food would be good, but I'm not up for anything big."

"That's fine. I'll go see what we can get."

She stopped, looking scared for a moment, and asked, "Where are you and Diesel staying?"

"We're right across the hallway."

"Good," she said, "I don't even know if I'll sleep tonight. Everything's been so messed up for so long."

"You'll sleep," he promised.

She rolled her eyes and said, "Says you." Walking to the bathtub, she put the plug in, turned on the water, dropped in some bath salts she found on the corner of the tub, and said, "If you happen to find a change of clothes, that would be lovely too."

"That might take a little longer, but I can do it," he said, outside the bathroom door, not quite shut between them.

"Aleah'll need something too, plus the baby."

"She's taken care of," he said. "I honestly didn't think about you needing clothes."

She snorted at that. "Right. What would I do? Walk around naked all the time?" When Shane went silent on the other side, she smiled. "Not happening."

"Are you sure?"

"I'm sure," she said. "It'll be too damn cold."

"Oh, I don't think you'll be cold anytime soon." Something in his voice had her peeking out of the bathroom and looking at him. "What do you mean?"

"We'll be too busy."

"Busy doing what?" she asked suspiciously.

But his expression was unreadable. He motioned at the hotel door and said, "I'll be back in a few."

The moment he walked out, she sank into the hot bath, moaning, as her multiple scrapes and bruises hit the hot water. But it felt so damn good. She closed her eyes and let her head sink under the water and then used the shampoo to soak and scrub her head several times—gently—but her head had stopped pounding thankfully. By the time she was done, she just lay in the heated, warm, secure blanket of a hot bath and enjoyed it.

When a knock came at the door, and it opened a crack, she said, "I sure hope that's Shane."

"It's me," he said.

"Good," she said in a sleepy voice. "Were you able to find me some clothes?"

"Some," he said. "I also found food."

"Does that mean I have to get out?"

Poking his head around the door, looking at her buried in the water, he smiled. "Doesn't look like you want to go anywhere just yet."

"I don't. I really don't," she said.

"I'm not sure you want to eat this in there though," he murmured.

"Is it pasta?"

He stared at her for a moment, then grinned and said, "What do you think?"

Her eyes popped open. "Okay, I'm getting out." Pulling the plug, she got out, dried off, wrapped herself in a towel, and stepped out into the room. "What did you get me for clothes?" she asked.

"Well," he said, "I found a few things." He pointed at a long robe, with a zipper in the front.

She quickly pulled that over her head, tugging the towel out from underneath, as he watched with interest. She just rolled her eyes at him. "Come on. Be a gentleman and don't look," she murmured.

"Well, if you won't change, why should I?" Then he sat down at the table and said, "Come and eat."

She walked over, inhaled the aroma, and smiled. "Now this," she said, "this is lovely."

"Exactly." She ate half of her dinner and then shook her head. "I'm too tired to eat it all."

"Then you can rest," he said. "Go to bed and just sleep. Unwind."

"I don't know," she said. "So many horrible things are in my mind right now that I don't even want to close my eyes, in case they take over."

"That's to be expected, considering all you've been

through." He stood and picked her up in one quick move, making her shriek, then walked to the window, where a big armchair was. He sat down with her in it. She curled up in his arms and whispered, "This is much better."

"It is," he said. "You know what? Ever since Diesel met you, he's been bugging me about why we weren't together."

"What did you tell him?"

"I said that we were good friends, and that it wasn't part of who we were."

"Interesting," she muttered, not liking the direction of the conversation.

"He told me that I was a fool and that I wasn't seeing what was right in front of me."

"Well, that's quite true," she said. "You are a fool."

He burst out laughing. "Maybe," he said, "but I'm a fast learner. One of the things that I've learned is that, when somebody tells me something, I need to pay attention."

"Yeah, and what did you need to pay attention to?" she murmured.

"You," he said, reaching up and tapping her nose. "And I realized that the reason we've been such good friends is because we really care about each other. We care at a level that most relationships never even get to. We've been friends for so long that we've seen the ins, the outs—the good, the bad, and the ugly. We've seen each other with relationships and breakups. We both came close to getting married to someone else at one point in time," he said. "And yet we didn't."

"Nope," she said, "it wasn't right."

"So how do you feel about things now?" he asked. "Does this feel right?"

She pushed herself up from his chest, looked at him quietly, and said, "You mean, being in your arms?"

He nodded.

"Yeah," she said, "it feels very right."

"And we've never really been the kind of people to worry so much about tomorrow," he said. "So, are you interested in seeing where this goes?"

"Yes," she said, and then she hesitated. "But I'll be pissed if it doesn't go where I want it to because then I'll have lost my best friend," she murmured.

His gaze deepened, and he said, "I don't see that happening." And he looked at her. "Unless you do."

"No," she said, "I don't. As long as you don't."

He burst out laughing. "And here we are," he said, "both of us walking around each other instead of saying exactly what we feel."

"No, you're right," she said. "I'd like to see where this goes."

He slid his arms along her back, tucked her close to him, and said, "Good, because I really do too."

"I thought you were the one who was holding back."

"Yeah," he said, "and then I realized that, when I think about all my journeys and missions—and who is on my mind when I get off work and where I want to go and who I think about when I want to talk about something—it's always you. I don't know why I didn't see it before. I don't know why I didn't see you," he said. "I presume we were just so busy living life and doing our own thing that it just never occurred to us to go that far."

"I can agree with that." She slid her arms around his neck and whispered, "So where does that leave us?"

"You know what? I think it leaves us as two people who have always loved each other, finally deciding to act on all those instincts kept submerged all this time."

She chuckled. "We've been very good at it."

"And maybe," he said, "it's just that the timing wasn't right for both of us in the past, and something about right now is perfect."

"I can accept that." She leaned forward and kissed him gently on his dimpled chin and then again on his cheek, her fingers gently flowing across to his other cheek, then coming down to brush her index finger against his lower lip. He immediately nibbled on her lip. She murmured, "Are you sure you're ready to do this?"

"Oh, hell, yes," he said. "I'm ready to do this."

She smiled and sat up on his lap, straddling him with one knee on either side. Cupping each side of his face with her hands, she kissed him deeply. His arms slipped around her waist, and he pulled her tighter against him. The kiss deepened into something so much darker than either had expected to develop so fast.

"It's like the passion has always been there," he murmured.

"I think it always was, but we took it for friendship," she said. "We took it for best-friend love. Because we were still each taking our lives in other directions." He kissed her again and again, then picked her up in his arms and carried her to the bed. "You're wearing too many clothes," she murmured.

He nodded. "And I should probably have a shower."

"Afterward," she said. He hesitated. She shook her head and said, "There's nothing about a warrior that I don't like, so get back down here."

Laughing, he said, "I thought I was wearing too many clothes." He pulled his shirt out of his pants and over his head, throwing it to the floor.

She immediately bounded to her knees, her hands exploring his chest, her fingers going to his belt buckle. By the time she had his jeans to his knees, her hands were already inside his boxers, cupping him.

He sucked in his breath. "You could take your time, you know?" he said, gasping.

"Oh, I intend to," she said. "We've got all night."

He groaned. "You'll be just as feisty in bed, won't you?"

"You wouldn't want me any other way," she murmured.

He laughed. "I think you're right. I want you just the way you've always been."

"It's a darn good thing," she said, "because that's exactly who I am, in bed and out."

He leaned forward and kissed her. As she slipped the boxers down over his hips, her hands circling around to cup his buttocks, he tried to kick out of his jeans, and he groaned. "I've still got my boots on, for Christ's sake."

She laughed and hopped off the bed, and, as he sat back down, she helped him get his boots and socks off. Then she pulled off the jeans and boxers. While he watched, she slowly lowered the zipper on her gown and stepped out of it, completely nude. She stood there in front of him and smiled. "You know what?" she said. "I don't think we've ever been in this state together before."

He shook his head. "Nope. Bathing suits, yes," he said, "but like this? Never."

She smiled, pushed him back on the bed and once again crawled up on his lap with one knee on either side of him. Only this time she teased the hard ridge of his erection.

He smiled, his hands on her hips. Then he stroked gently up her ribs and across her breasts, gently cupping one and then the other, his thumb sliding over the nipples, up to her collarbone, and onto her neck.

She smiled, leaned down, and kissed him gently.

He pulled her closer, so their tongues could war, as the passion between them once again climbed, albeit a little slower. She slid back and forth against his shaft, still teasing him, and her, moaning with pleasure. He gripped her hips and whispered, "That'll make things a little too fast."

"A little too fast is just fine right now."

He groaned, as she kept up the movement. He whispered, "You could at least do that another way."

She smiled and whispered, "Like this?" And she raised herself up, positioned his shaft, and slowly sank down on him. He groaned, his hips pushing upward into her, as she controlled the movement. By the time she was fully seated, or at least thought she was, she sat down and ground her hips against him.

He gasped, holding her hips and twisting beneath her. She reached behind to gently cup the globes and to stroke the softness between his thighs. He shuddered underneath her, and she watched the passion twist across his face, as his hands gripped her hips hard.

She slid her hands along his forearms to his shoulders and then braced herself and asked, "You ready to ride?"

"Nobody would ever say no to that offer."

Slowly she lifted herself up the velvet shaft and then slid back down, up and then down, the pace increasing with every movement. Again and again she moved her hips frantically, as she drove toward the pleasure they both awaited, his hands trying to not force his own rhythm, until she cried out.

And, when she finally did and threw her head back, sitting tall astride him, he murmured, "Shelly, you are so beautiful. I think I just glimpsed Valhalla."

And the explosions rocked through her.

He quickly flipped her, threw her heels atop his shoulders, and he pounded into her, driving for his own pleasure. When he finally exploded within her, she felt another set of cataclysmic explosions, sending her off again. By the time he collapsed beside her, she shuddered in joy and delight.

He wrapped her up tight, held her close, and whispered, "My God," he said. "I had no idea something like that was possible between us," he said. "We should have gotten here a hell of a long time ago."

"Maybe so," she said, "but I can tell you that it was well worth waiting for."

He wrapped her in his arms, pulling her closer, and said, "And we have a lifetime."

"Thank God," she said, "I'm really glad to be done with that stage of life."

He burst out laughing. "What stage?"

"The dating stage," she said. "Who knew that my handsome hero actually was my best friend?"

"Well, your best friend didn't," he muttered, holding her close.

"Fools, the both of us," she said, laughing.

"That's all right," he said. "We got it now."

And he kissed her again, and she had to agree. What they had now was worth everything they'd been through together to get here. She smiled, wrapped her arms around him, and whispered, "Did I ever tell you that I love you?"

"Yes," he said, "many times."

"Well, it's true," she said, "even more so today than any other. For I'm in love with you."

He nodded and whispered against her ear gently, "And I

love you, and I'm in love with you too."

She smiled, closed her eyes, and said, "Now I'll nap for a bit. Wake me up in a little while."

"No, I'll let you sleep."

"Either you wake me up or I'll wake you."

"Well, whoever wakes up first gets to wake the other," he said, stifling a yawn.

She chuckled, tucked in against him, and soon fell asleep, with a smile on her face and with the promise of a peaceful night ahead of her, as she stepped into her new life with Shane.

EPILOGUE

D IESEL EDWARDS WALKED back into his small apartment, even as his cell phone rang inside. He quickly picked it up and answered. It was Shane. "Hey, I was just outside, washing the car."

"And you didn't have your phone on you?"

"No," he said. "Sometimes I just don't want to be connected."

"Got it," he said.

"How are you two getting along?"

"Well, Shelly's back here in California, and we're looking for apartments right now," he said. "She's looking for a job but not pushing it."

"I wouldn't push it either. Her last job was a bit of a killer."

At that, Shane snorted. "You think? They did give her a nice severance package though, hoping that they wouldn't get sued for the lack of security. But, all in all, we're doing great."

"Perfect," he said.

"What about you?" Shane said.

"Yeah, I'm back, normal, recovered," he said. "I had a few days of rest."

"That's good."

"Just a check-up call?"

"Well, I would invite you over for a barbecue," he said, "but …"

"But?" Diesel walked to the small balcony and stepped out. He was just on the outskirts of San Diego, and the smog was not too bad today, but it was pretty muggy. "So, you got a job for me or what?"

"Well, it's not me who's got a job for you. The Mavericks do."

"My own job?" Diesel asked in surprise.

"Yeah, if you're up for it."

"Any reason I wouldn't be?"

"I'm not sure," he said. "How do you feel about scientists?"

"No different than any other person. Why?"

"Because a specialist, an epidemiologist, has been kidnapped."

"And that's a Mavericks issue, why?"

"She was working on a new cure for a virus. Apparently China is looking to have the cure for themselves, and she is their best bet."

"Is it part of that H1N1 that's terrorizing Asia?"

"It's one of the offshoots of it," he said. "Anyway, she went missing twelve days ago."

"Why are we getting called in so late?"

"Because her family didn't report her missing."

"What family would that be?"

"Her brother, who lives with her. When he finally did call it in, nobody really believed him because he was drunk."

"Great, so how believable is her disappearance?"

"We checked the street cams, and two Asian males clearly escorted her, as soon as she left her home, into a black car."

"And?"

"It went to the Chinese Consulate. However, the consulate is saying that nobody arrived."

"Did you show them the video?"

"Yes, but they say the car isn't theirs, and honestly the camera doesn't go clear onto their property."

"So, what are the chances that she was even taken by the Chinese?" he said. "It's pretty easy to blame them by taking her to that location but then sneak her off somewhere else."

"Yes, it's quite possible," he said, "which is why you're being called in for it."

"And what's the problem?"

"Well, I think at the moment she's on a Chinese warship."

"How did we go from the Chinese Consulate *not* having anything to do with it to a Chinese warship?"

"Well, it gets better than that," he said. "Her last sighting was on a Chinese junk boat."

"Where?"

"Off China's coast."

"That's not making any sense."

"Nope, we'll fill you in as you go," he said cheerfully.

"Go where?"

"To the last sighting of her. How are your language skills? Like Chinese, possibly Vietnamese?"

"Terrible," he said, "I suck at it, but things always work out." As they spoke, he was already pulling out a duffel bag and packing up his clothes. He heard a vehicle outside and shook his head. "Are you telling me that that I'm leaving right now?"

"Aren't you packed yet? You should have started when I first called."

"I might have, if we hadn't been talking about you guys and a barbecue that you owe me," he said. Nonetheless he was packed within minutes.

"Make sure you've got your passport."

"I've got it," he said. "I still don't understand why this scientist was kidnapped."

"Well, she's got a scientific background for one. She's a renowned epidemiologist for another, and she's got some head start on a cure for this ... this virus."

"That's great, but then somebody wants her for a lab, right?"

"Well, that's what we're hoping for, but, of course, it could just as easily be extortion."

"And we don't know."

"Well, that's for you to find out," he said. "In the meantime, we're still tracking her movements. Please bring her home." And, with that, Shane went to log off.

"Wait," Diesel said, "when am I leaving?"

"I thought I made it clear that you're supposed to be packing."

"Not only am I packed, I've locked up my apartment, and I'm standing outside."

"Oh, well, do you see the little red car parked in front of you?"

He looked at the parking lot and found it. There appeared to be no driver. "Yeah?"

"The keys are under the floor mat."

"Where am I going?"

"Head to Coronado base. You'll take a little bit of a convoluted route."

"Why is that?"

"Because the Chinese government says they don't know

214

anything about it, yet they're obviously involved. So we're staying under the radar."

"Hey, that's ... we've still got to get there fast."

"Yep. Don't worry. You'll get there fast. Your flight's leaving in about forty minutes. Make sure you're on it."

And, with a laugh, he hung up, leaving Diesel to hop into the little red Mustang and to hurtle toward the airport on the base. He didn't know whose car this was, but it was a hell of a way to leave town.

And, with that thought uppermost in his mind, he hit the gas and went forward to whatever life would bring.

This concludes Book 12 of The Mavericks: Shane.

Read about Diesel: The Mavericks, Book 13

The Mavericks: Diesel (Book #13)

What happens when the very men—trained to make the hard decisions—come up against the rules and regulations that hold them back from doing what needs to be done? They either stay and work within the constraints given to them or they walk away. Only now, for a select few, they have another option:

The Mavericks. A covert black ops team that steps up and break all the rules … but gets the job done.

Welcome to a new military romance series by *USA Today* best-selling author Dale Mayer. A series where you meet new friends and just might get to meet old ones too in this raw and compelling look at the men who keep us safe every day from the darkness where they operate—and live—in the shadows … until someone special helps them step into the light.

Traveling to China to retrieve a kidnapped scientist shows Diesel the depths of human depravity. Not that he needs more proof. He's been doing this type of work for a decade. This is the first time though the person he was rescuing was this interesting.

Eva Langston had been kidnapped while walking across the street and then locked up in a lab half a world away. Joining two other scientists, both letting her know there was no escape, she refuses to give up hope. When the rescue does come, it wasn't smooth or easy.

Still she was damn glad to be free. Until she realizes that freedom is a long way off, as, one by one, her science team is picked off, leaving her the last one to be dealt with.

Author's Note

Thank you for reading Shane: The Mavericks, Book 12! If you enjoyed the book, please take a moment and leave a short review.

Dear reader,

I love to hear from readers, and you can contact me at my website: www.dalemayer.com or at my Facebook author page. To be informed of new releases and special offers, sign up for my newsletter or follow me on BookBub. And if you are interested in joining Dale Mayer's Reader Group, here is the Facebook sign up page.
https://smarturl.it/DaleMayerFBGroup

Cheers,
Dale Mayer

Get THREE Free Books Now!

Have you met the SEALS of Honor?

SEALs of Honor Books 1, 2, and 3. Follow the stories of brave, badass warriors who serve their country with honor and love their women to the limits of life and death.

Read Mason, Hawk, and Dane right now for FREE.

Go here and tell me where to send them!
http://smarturl.it/EthanBofB

About the Author

Dale Mayer is a USA Today bestselling author best known for her Psychic Visions and Family Blood Ties series. Her contemporary romances are raw and full of passion and emotion (Second Chances, SKIN), her thrillers will keep you guessing (By Death series), and her romantic comedies will keep you giggling (It's a Dog's Life and Charmin Marvin Romantic Comedy series).

She honors the stories that come to her – and some of them are crazy and break all the rules and cross multiple genres!

To go with her fiction, she also writes nonfiction in many different fields with books available on resume writing, companion gardening and the US mortgage system. She has recently published her Career Essentials Series. All her books are available in print and ebook format.

Connect with Dale Mayer Online

Dale's Website – www.dalemayer.com
Facebook Personal – https://smarturl.it/DaleMayerFacebook
Instagram – https://smarturl.it/DaleMayerInstagram
BookBub – https://smarturl.it/DaleMayerBookbub
Facebook Fan Page – https://smarturl.it/DaleMayerFBFanPage
Goodreads – https://smarturl.it/DaleMayerGoodreads

Also by Dale Mayer

Published Adult Books:

Hathaway House
Aaron, Book 1
Brock, Book 2
Cole, Book 3
Denton, Book 4
Elliot, Book 5
Finn, Book 6
Gregory, Book 7
Heath, Book 8
Iain, Book 9
Jaden, Book 10
Keith, Book 11
Lance, Book 12
Melissa, Book 13
Nash, Book 14
Owen, Book 15
Hathaway House, Books 1–3
Hathaway House, Books 4–6
Hathaway House, Books 7–9

The K9 Files
Ethan, Book 1
Pierce, Book 2
Zane, Book 3

Blaze, Book 4

Lucas, Book 5

Parker, Book 6

Carter, Book 7

Weston, Book 8

Greyson, Book 9

Rowan, Book 10

Caleb, Book 11

Kurt, Book 12

Tucker, Book 13

Harley, Book 14

The K9 Files, Books 1–2

The K9 Files, Books 3–4

The K9 Files, Books 5–6

The K9 Files, Books 7–8

The K9 Files, Books 9–10

The K9 Files, Books 11–12

Lovely Lethal Gardens

Arsenic in the Azaleas, Book 1

Bones in the Begonias, Book 2

Corpse in the Carnations, Book 3

Daggers in the Dahlias, Book 4

Evidence in the Echinacea, Book 5

Footprints in the Ferns, Book 6

Gun in the Gardenias, Book 7

Handcuffs in the Heather, Book 8

Ice Pick in the Ivy, Book 9

Jewels in the Juniper, Book 10

Killer in the Kiwis, Book 11

Lifeless in the Lilies, Book 12

Lovely Lethal Gardens, Books 1–2

Lovely Lethal Gardens, Books 3–4
Lovely Lethal Gardens, Books 5–6
Lovely Lethal Gardens, Books 7–8
Lovely Lethal Gardens, Books 9–10

Psychic Vision Series
Tuesday's Child
Hide 'n Go Seek
Maddy's Floor
Garden of Sorrow
Knock Knock…
Rare Find
Eyes to the Soul
Now You See Her
Shattered
Into the Abyss
Seeds of Malice
Eye of the Falcon
Itsy-Bitsy Spider
Unmasked
Deep Beneath
From the Ashes
Stroke of Death
Ice Maiden
Psychic Visions Books 1–3
Psychic Visions Books 4–6
Psychic Visions Books 7–9

By Death Series
Touched by Death
Haunted by Death
Chilled by Death
By Death Books 1–3

Broken Protocols – Romantic Comedy Series
Cat's Meow
Cat's Pajamas
Cat's Cradle
Cat's Claus
Broken Protocols 1-4

Broken and… Mending
Skin
Scars
Scales (of Justice)
Broken but… Mending 1-3

Glory
Genesis
Tori
Celeste
Glory Trilogy

Biker Blues
Morgan: Biker Blues, Volume 1
Cash: Biker Blues, Volume 2

SEALs of Honor
Mason: SEALs of Honor, Book 1
Hawk: SEALs of Honor, Book 2
Dane: SEALs of Honor, Book 3
Swede: SEALs of Honor, Book 4
Shadow: SEALs of Honor, Book 5
Cooper: SEALs of Honor, Book 6
Markus: SEALs of Honor, Book 7
Evan: SEALs of Honor, Book 8
Mason's Wish: SEALs of Honor, Book 9

Chase: SEALs of Honor, Book 10
Brett: SEALs of Honor, Book 11
Devlin: SEALs of Honor, Book 12
Easton: SEALs of Honor, Book 13
Ryder: SEALs of Honor, Book 14
Macklin: SEALs of Honor, Book 15
Corey: SEALs of Honor, Book 16
Warrick: SEALs of Honor, Book 17
Tanner: SEALs of Honor, Book 18
Jackson: SEALs of Honor, Book 19
Kanen: SEALs of Honor, Book 20
Nelson: SEALs of Honor, Book 21
Taylor: SEALs of Honor, Book 22
Colton: SEALs of Honor, Book 23
Troy: SEALs of Honor, Book 24
Axel: SEALs of Honor, Book 25
Baylor: SEALs of Honor, Book 26
SEALs of Honor, Books 1–3
SEALs of Honor, Books 4–6
SEALs of Honor, Books 7–10
SEALs of Honor, Books 11–13
SEALs of Honor, Books 14–16
SEALs of Honor, Books 17–19
SEALs of Honor, Books 20–22
SEALs of Honor, Books 23–25

Heroes for Hire

Levi's Legend: Heroes for Hire, Book 1
Stone's Surrender: Heroes for Hire, Book 2
Merk's Mistake: Heroes for Hire, Book 3
Rhodes's Reward: Heroes for Hire, Book 4
Flynn's Firecracker: Heroes for Hire, Book 5

Logan's Light: Heroes for Hire, Book 6

Harrison's Heart: Heroes for Hire, Book 7

Saul's Sweetheart: Heroes for Hire, Book 8

Dakota's Delight: Heroes for Hire, Book 9

Michael's Mercy (Part of Sleeper SEAL Series)

Tyson's Treasure: Heroes for Hire, Book 10

Jace's Jewel: Heroes for Hire, Book 11

Rory's Rose: Heroes for Hire, Book 12

Brandon's Bliss: Heroes for Hire, Book 13

Liam's Lily: Heroes for Hire, Book 14

North's Nikki: Heroes for Hire, Book 15

Anders's Angel: Heroes for Hire, Book 16

Reyes's Raina: Heroes for Hire, Book 17

Dezi's Diamond: Heroes for Hire, Book 18

Vince's Vixen: Heroes for Hire, Book 19

Ice's Icing: Heroes for Hire, Book 20

Johan's Joy: Heroes for Hire, Book 21

Galen's Gemma: Heroes for Hire, Book 22

Zack's Zest: Heroes for Hire, Book 23

Bonaparte's Belle: Heroes for Hire, Book 24

Heroes for Hire, Books 1–3

Heroes for Hire, Books 4–6

Heroes for Hire, Books 7–9

Heroes for Hire, Books 10–12

Heroes for Hire, Books 13–15

SEALs of Steel

Badger: SEALs of Steel, Book 1

Erick: SEALs of Steel, Book 2

Cade: SEALs of Steel, Book 3

Talon: SEALs of Steel, Book 4

Laszlo: SEALs of Steel, Book 5

Geir: SEALs of Steel, Book 6

Jager: SEALs of Steel, Book 7

The Final Reveal: SEALs of Steel, Book 8

SEALs of Steel, Books 1–4

SEALs of Steel, Books 5–8

SEALs of Steel, Books 1–8

The Mavericks

Kerrick, Book 1

Griffin, Book 2

Jax, Book 3

Beau, Book 4

Asher, Book 5

Ryker, Book 6

Miles, Book 7

Nico, Book 8

Keane, Book 9

Lennox, Book 10

Gavin, Book 11

Shane, Book 12

Diesel, Book 13

The Mavericks, Books 1–2

The Mavericks, Books 3–4

The Mavericks, Books 5–6

The Mavericks, Books 7–8

The Mavericks, Books 9–10

The Mavericks, Books 11–12

Bullard's Battle Series

Ryland's Reach, Book 1

Cain's Cross, Book 2

Eton's Escape, Book 3

Garret's Gambit, Book 4

Kano's Keep, Book 5
Fallon's Flaw, Book 6
Quinn's Quest, Book 7
Bullard's Beauty, Book 8

Collections
Dare to Be You…
Dare to Love…
Dare to be Strong…
RomanceX3

Standalone Novellas
It's a Dog's Life
Riana's Revenge
Second Chances

Published Young Adult Books:

Family Blood Ties Series
Vampire in Denial
Vampire in Distress
Vampire in Design
Vampire in Deceit
Vampire in Defiance
Vampire in Conflict
Vampire in Chaos
Vampire in Crisis
Vampire in Control
Vampire in Charge
Family Blood Ties Set 1–3
Family Blood Ties Set 1–5
Family Blood Ties Set 4–6
Family Blood Ties Set 7–9

Sian's Solution, A Family Blood Ties Series Prequel
Novelette

Design series
Dangerous Designs
Deadly Designs
Darkest Designs
Design Series Trilogy

Standalone
In Cassie's Corner
Gem Stone (a Gemma Stone Mystery)
Time Thieves

Published Non-Fiction Books:

Career Essentials
Career Essentials: The Résumé
Career Essentials: The Cover Letter
Career Essentials: The Interview
Career Essentials: 3 in 1

Made in the USA
Coppell, TX
30 January 2021

49179305R00131